WOMEN IN SCRUB

IN SCRUB

MILES H. PLOWDEN, III

iUniverse®

WOMEN IN SCRUB

iUniverse books may be ordered through booksellers or by contacting:

iUniverse
1663 Liberty Drive
Bloomington, IN 47403
www.iuniverse.com
1-800-Authors (1-800-288-4677)

Because of the dynamic nature of the Internet, any web addresses or links contained in this book may have changed since publication and may no longer be valid. The views expressed in this work are solely those of the author and do not necessarily reflect the views of the publisher, and the publisher hereby disclaims any responsibility for them.

Any people depicted in stock imagery provided by Getty Images are models, and such images are being used for illustrative purposes only. Certain stock imagery © Getty Images.

ISBN: 978-1-5320-7424-0 (sc)
ISBN: 978-1-5320-7426-4 (hc)
ISBN: 978-1-5320-7425-7 (e)

Print information available on the last page.

iUniverse rev. date: 05/29/2019

DEDICATION

This dedication is easier to write for it involves my wife Carolyn M. Plowden and my good friend and Mentor Phyllis Gilbert, who is in charge of the Winter Haven Heritage Association. She is keeping the history of Winter Haven in front of our eyes and though the youth of this nation has been blinded by the lack of learning about history. They will be the ones who can and may study what persons like Phyllis Gilbert has preserved for them.

Both of these ladies have kept me busy adding words to the page and watching very close if I get out of rhythm they quickly pull me back to the outline.

Mr. Bob Gernert, Executive Secretary of the Winter Haven, Florida Chamber of Commerce, digs out the time from his busy schedule, to also fine tunes the Winter Haven Museum, at much personal expense to himself finding artifacts that apply to Winter Haven from antique postcards to a Seminole Indian dug out canoe. I find the best part is that he has opened the way for me to be part on the Museum and through that venue has come these books which I have written. I cannot thank Bob Gernert enough for his service to Winter Haven and Polk County, Florida, and to the amount of time he has spent helping me with things that he really should not have been bothered with.

ACKNOWLEDGMENT

I would like to acknowledge the people who are there assisting me in every effort to write these lines, who make the suggestions, and even work building the cover like the cover for <u>WOMEN IN THE SCRUB; Long Days and Hard Work</u>, was done by Karen Starling of: DREAM BUILDERS DESIGNS, Bartow, Florida, (www. DreamBuilderDesign. com). Karen provides graphic and web site development services. She also created Cover Art for my first book, <u>CRACKERS IN THE SCRUB; ADVENTURES AND STORIES ABOUT FLORIDA CRACKER COWBOYS.</u>

My mentor and wonderful friend Phyllis Gilbert, who keeps me checking for my own errors, punctuation and grammar. (I should have had her when I was taking high school English, not to mention college English).

My wonderful wife Carolyn M. Plowden, who would read the rough drafts and with her trusty red pencil would make the pages look as though they had been in one of the shoot outs in the body of the book. Red was everywhere on the page and I would retype the page or correct it in the computer. She would stay up late at night "grading" my book chapter by chapter until it was the best we could do, and now it is up to the editor of these pages to make them ready for the publisher.

PREFACE

WOMEN IN THE SCRUB; Long Days and Hard Work, is a historical fiction about Florida cracker women, in the late 1800s. Maude Elsie Tanner and Spurgeon Tanner ran the stagecoach line that brought passengers, mail and the Wells Fargo strong box from Ft. Cummins to the Bent Penny ranch, to the stage depot at Tanners settlement where Spurgeon and Maude Elsie also ran a general store. The final leg of the stagecoach was through Bartow and terminated at Tampa. The depot was the wayside inn for the traveler who was on the stagecoach, horse and buggy, buckboard wagon, afoot, or on horse back. Rooms were rented, food was served boarding house style. Other women became part of the Tanner settlement. Savannah Ford who was a good nurse as well as a wonderful cook. Nadine who gave birth to triplets, Tomega who was an Indian wet nurse for the triplets. The story flows, and life carried on, with the help of all the guests and friends through happiness and sadness, the years move forward, balanced and waiting for the world of the Florida scrub to create the next big surprise.

This work has mystery, romance, child birth and gun fights, and guileful Seminole

Indian women. The vernacular of the old cracker dialog is prevalent that makes an interesting read. The primitive conditions are countered with strong determination and will. They would eventually create a land where folks such as these independent pioneers, made the lives of the future settlers more bearable through taming the rugged Florida frontier. So with hard work and a bit of luck these WOMEN IN THE SCRUB; Long Days and Hard Work, were exemplary in grubbing an existence for the cracker cowboy, to make the scrub less miserable and kept the lamp burning in the window for him to come home, even late at night.

FOREWORD

"Long Days and Hard Work is no idiom for the words are true and if any woman from the Twenty-first century were to suddenly find herself in the latter days of the nineteenth century; hardly a man would be found that would understand why this throughly modern woman would after no less than one week be found dead hanging from an oak tree in the scrub a victim of her own mortal hand.

The woman from the nineteenth century would find that the chores of that day were the norm of that day; the norm of the woman of the twenty-first century would find boiling clothes in a wash pot and boiling starch on a wood fired stove and starching and hanging the laundry on a clothes line, ironing with a flat iron heated from the same wood burning stove, rather than placing them in an automatic clothes drier would be more than she could live with and thus the rope, oak tree, and demise of the modern woman.

This is a series of stories about the men and women coming out of the nineteenth century and what a serious event it was.

The stories are true, the names are fictitious, and the facts are spelled out as best that the author can relate them to the reader. Though it is about WOMEN IN THE SCRUB, Long Days and Hard Work; did not end at sundown for the women as for the men there were still plenty of chores to do before the lady's hair was wrapped and she could place her head upon her pillow for the night. Then her day started again at four-thirty in the morning to have breakfast on the table so that the men could get "an early start on the day."

All names are fictitious, places are historically real and will be recognized by a lot of folks in Polk County, and are explained in the "character chart" in the front of this book. Thank you for the time you take reading this book because I wrote it for your enjoyment. Miles.

CONTENTS

CHARACTER CHART

Maude Elsie, Tanner

The matriarch of the Tanner clan. A lady in her late fifties who is tanned and aged with the hard work of eking out a living as a pioneer wife, mother, nurse and minister of good will to family and friends.

Spurgeon Tanner

The Father, husband of Maude Elsie, a man in his early fifties with hard features, skin was so dark tanned it appeared to be leather. Ice blue eyes that didn't seem to belong in that face, he was a cow and hog hunter. The proprietor of the Tanner Stage Lines and Depot, the owner of the Tanner's General Store, and a wise sage of the scrub.

Spurgeon Borkman Tanner, Jr.

The first born of the Tanner house hold when there was hardly anything but scrub and a lean to and later a Chickee which the Indians taught the Tanners to build. Schooled in the scrub he attended the University of Florida school of business His blonde hair, fair complexion and smooth demeanor always attracted the opposite sex.

Thomas Tanner

The second son of Maude Elsie and Spurgeon Tanner, who all of his life was a tinkerer and loved to restore antiques. Was educated in the U. S. Army where he retired and later discovered rich treasures in his fathers barn. He was rugged and tall at nearly six feet with strong features. His hazel eyes were from his mother his strong chin, from his father, his red hair was his own.

Seth Michael Tanner

The third and last son of the Tanners and two years younger than Thomas and four years younger than Spurgeon, Jr. He was the prodical son as he went away at age sixteen and worked at saw mills and terpentine stills until one led him back to the Tanners Settlement.

The Stage Depot

Later became a boarding house when the stage line was replaced by the railroad.

General Store

Tanner's found a lacking of being so far from the towns that a general store was built to accommodate the local people, Indians, and stagecoach travelers.

Joe "Mossy Back" Tuttle

The chief stagecoach driver and mechanic of the stage line. A man about fifty with long gray hair that strung out from under his hat and waved in the wind as he drove the stage. His clothes were denim breeches with home spun shirt and a buck skin vest. He carried a colt pistol and fifty rounds of ammunition in his belt. No one ever successfully robbed a coach he was driving.

Efrim Johnson

Efrim had no middle name and was the assistant stage driver and shot gun rider. He was a five foot burned out cowboy who looked like a tired old man with glasses and a full beard that he would tuck inside his shirt when he ate. His kind brown eyes plead for a peaceful time at all occasions.

The widow Longberry

The owner of a café hotel and bar in Tampa, where Mossy Back and Efrim often stayed over night if she kept a room for them.

Savannah Ford

A beautiful young, blonde lady with long tresses nearly to her waist. She had a past secret and needed to find herself. Who decided that the stagecoach was not the way she wanted to travel yet became attached to the depot boarding house and to the Tanners

Dirk Richards
Savannah's suitor who was absorbed by the scrub, but not her.

Stanley "Mel" Melrose
The county sheriff and peace officer of the scrub. He was a pudgy man with a bald head and whiskers of a four day growth. His face would turn red if he got riled which was often the case. He was good at solving cases.

Claude Hayman
A young handsome fellow from the Western Union office who was setting up the telegraph offices in the area for better communications about the county. He was tall and tan from being on the line crew in the Florida sun, he was educated at a college in Georgia, and came to Florida to survey for the Western Union.

Russell Workman
A young newly wed and father to be, who went astray in an unfortunate way.

Nadine Workman
The wife of Russell and a very pretty, small lady who was found in a strange situation as she tried to relocate at the Tanners boarding house. Petite in stature but had huge culinary skills, for a woman in the scrub.

Hans Nuddleman
A German Jew who owned the Sawmill where most of the lumber and jobs outside of being a Cracker Cowboy were held.

James Bray
Olivia Bray, and two children were found living in the home that Nadine and Russell had started. As squatters the times were rough on the family.

Doc Zimmerman

The kindly "Ole Doc" of the scrub. Wore a black wool suit with a bow tie, his hair was silver gray and his buggy was black with a white horse pulling it through the scrub. He was tall, over six feet and had a grand bedside manner, with his smooth talk and nerve easing speech.

Tomega (Toe- Meg-Ah)

A Seminole woman who was an Indian midwife, and a wet nurse who would feed small babies, mothers milk when the natural mother could not feed the child. She was round and tender, she was dark skinned and her black hair did not look natural her deep blue eyes were different from the normal brown eyes of the Indians. She was good with herbs, roots, berries and teas to mend the sick person.

Professor Tillman Clark

A wandering minstrel, who with his steam powered calliope was the music man of the scrub. He was tall, wore a split tail coat, top hat, white shirt and string bow tie, he played practically every musical instrument known to man. He had one failing which was a poor choice for the music man.

The Seven Prisoners

Martin Sobol, the old man of fifty, and father to three of the men in the gang, James Sobol the oldest son of twenty-five, Henry Sobol the middle son aged twenty-one, John Gary Sobol, the youngest at age eighteen. The rest of the gang were: Burt Chinfry, age twenty-two, a hateful man with squinted eyes, many facial scars from old fights and slashes. Aleck Ed Genery, age twenty-three already an escapee from a Texas jail for murder and other mayhem with orders to be hanged. Daneen Maddock, the outlaw's outlaw, abused as a young lad and now age twenty-seven has had two decades to practice his own brand of cruelty to other people. All of these men were gun fighters of ruthless character.

Women In The Scrub

Maude Elsie Tanner, had worked for Mary Remmick and Brittany Crocket at the Bent Penny Ranch for several years. Her husband, Spurgeon Tanner, kept the stagecoach line and the general store in business. They had come to the area from Johnson City in eastern Tennessee, after selling the large emporium left to him by his father, and started up the small general store and the stage line from Tampa to Fort Cummins, where it connected with the railroad. It took nearly every cent he had to buy the horses, the rolling stock, and hire men to drive the stagecoaches. The passengers, a small contract to carry the U. S. Mail and Wells Fargo bank transfers of gold and paper cash strong box, was not enough income for the line, so to make ends meet Spurgeon, was having to round up what scrub cattle he could to sell. He butchered some along with hogs, to supply meat to the depots along the trace and there were always plenty of wild chickens for eggs and eating.

On a bright hot Florida summer day, Maude Elsie Tanner stood beside the lane shading her eyes as she looked toward the east and the cloud of dust being stirred up by the approaching stagecoach. As usual it was late but this time it was two hours behind and the ready team had been harnessed for all this time. Maude Elsie was thinking that the west bound stagecoach would be pulling in just any minute. Now they would need watering again before they could be hitched to the stage for their ten-mile run from here at the Bent Penny Trace and Tanner's store and stage depot to the next stop at Bartow.

Maude Elsie flipped her bonnet back over her red hair and used it to shade her eyes as she walked back to the ready corral. Watering the horses again meant carrying buckets of water to the horses rather than them drinking from the trough. "More work and back ache to carry buckets of water to that team," Maude Elsie thought as she walked back to the corner of the corral where the pump and buckets were. The eight horse team looked up at her familiar figure and snorted their approval at the smell of fresh water being pumped. She dutifully pumped two buckets and set them before the lead pair and when they had drunk their fill the next pair got their buckets of water. Timing was everything for as the last empty buckets were picked up from the ground the lead team relieved themselves of the water they had earlier drunk from the trough.

After the long pulls of cool water, each horse waited at the gang tree where they would be hitched; then the tree would be fastened with the king pin in the gang tree socket to form the shaft of the stagecoach.

The gang tree was a long round pole which had arms like branches of a tree; at a horse and a half length side-by-side with single trees attached to the branches. Only the lead horses had reins but were always run to the horse behind them so there could be no run-away. If the lead horses were reined to the right, then the tether would pull the second row of horses and make them turn right or "gee" with the others. This hitch was especially good for the sand ruts that made up most of the Florida trails in the 1890's, as it was created to allow each horse to pull at the same rate and added power to tow the heavy stagecoach.

Joe "Mossy Back" Tuttle was the driver and Efrim Johnson the box rider or shot gun on the incoming stage as it rattled, clinked, groaned and stirred up more dust. Then it pulled to a stop in front of the Tanner depot.

"All out-ya got fifteen minutes to do what ever hit aire you got to do in tha time hit takes ta re-hitch tha team." Mossy Back yelled at the passengers.

"Yew wimin kin use the privy but yew fellars got to go ta tha woods."

He continued to yell as he climbed down from the seat atop the stagecoach.

"Af-noon miz Maude Elsie, how's tha family? Spurgeon still a ailin wid tha broke arm still?" Then he added without giving her a chance to answer, "Yew dun watered them critters and they need to run fer a spell, they gonna slosh, ah recc'n."

"Yes sir, Mr. Tuttle, they have been watered just before you drove up and I am fine and no, Mr. Tanner has been over his broken arm for months now. He's out in the scrub with three of the boys and the dogs trying to round up some scrub cows or hogs to fatten for the winter. He should be back before dark, but you all will be to Bartow before he gets in, I guess," she answered with the same staccato that the questions were asked.

Efrim and Mossy Back hitched up the horses and led the old team to the corral where they each drank from the water trough until it was almost empty.

"Efrim, yew pump fer miz Maude Elsie and see to it them hoss critters git all they kin drank er else yew gotta buy at the Wider Longberry's tonight."

A whip cracked and a dog barked. As it did the three men who were on the stagecoach ran from the woods and hastened into the confines of the coach as Spurgeon and the boys along with the dogs, came into the lane from the scrub to the south of their farm. The dogs went to the stagecoach and barked at the strangers as Spurgeon whistled and cracked his fifteen-foot whip again and the dogs went back and drove the cows into the barn corral.

Spurgeon stepped down from his Marsh Tackie horse and nodded at Mossy Back and Efrim.

"Kicked fifteen head outen tha scrub t'day, aint seed no hogs," Spurgeon told Maude Elsie.

"That's good Spurgeon," she answered. "That makes an even hundred for the last two weeks. You can drive them over to the Bent Penny cow pens before long. Or are you going to fatten these to butcher this winter?"

"I'll fatten two or three, but the rest we need to sell." he answered Maude Elsie.

"Hey Tanner" Mossy Back called to Spurgeon and without answering Spurgeon turned and walked toward the corral.

Spurgeon walked up to the stage driver and asked. "What is it Mossy?" he looked to see if the hitch was going ok and when he looked back the driver was grinning at him.

"Did yew see that thar female lady Whuts ah got wid me this trip?" Mossy asked.

"Well no ah haint had hardly time ta go a lookin at no female lady. Ah jist got outen tha scrub and ah been a talkin ta Maude Elsie," Spurgeon answered.

"She's a looker I reccon she's the most looksumest female lady ah had in ma coach ever," Mossy said with a giggle.

"Well whar aire she at, ah reccon ah'm a gonna git looked at anyhow might is well be guilty as to git 'cuesed o' hit," Spurgeon told Mossy.

"Whut yall a palaverin bout?" Efrim stepped up to the huddle and asked.

"We's jist talkin bout at aire purty lady whuts a ridden wid us ishere trip." Mossy answered.

"Yep, she's a looker awe 'right," Efrim said. Then added, "The teams hitched and the old'uns is dun un-harnessed and watered and the trough is pumped full agin."

Efrim climbed up to the driver's seat and took up the cow horn and blew it three times and then shouted, "All aboard."

Spurgeon watched as the two ladies were helped into the coach by two of the men, then all three men climbed in and slammed the door. Efrim tooted the cows horn twice more and Mossy Back cracked his whip and away the eight horse team went with the stagecoach in tow.

Spurgeon started for the dooryard and then before the dust had settled from the departure of the stagecoach, he heard Efrim blowing his horn in short toots. He knew that meant trouble so he jumped on his little horse and whistled for the dogs. The dogs came out from under the front porch and ran as hard as they could to catch up with Spurgeon.

Spurgeon found the coach stopped on the trail and three men with bandanas over their face, one of them with an old Walker Colt in his hand. Before they saw Spurgeon coming up, the three wheeled their horses with their back toward him. He pointed the dogs at the men and said "Sic em_" The dogs each caught a horse by the nose, and as the horse reared the dogs were lifted up in the air but held on until the horses fell backward on top of its helpless rider. The one with the pistol didn't know what to do and was blind sided with a fifteen-foot cow whip which burned the old pistol from his hand. The next crack of the whip wrapped around the man's belly and with a smart tug of the whip he, came off his horse.

By this time Efrim had jumped from the stage seat and was covering the three fallen bandits with his double barrel shot gun. The dogs did not let them move either.

Spurgeon took his plaited rawhide riata, made a noose, and told the men to stand up.

They didn't want to move because of the dogs. Spurgeon whistled the dogs off and told them to heel. Two of the men got up but the third just lay there. He had broken his back in the fall from the frightened horse and was unable to speak also.

Spurgeon and Mossy made a travois for the man, and with his horse brought him to the depot. The others were made to climb atop the stagecoach and were made fast there until they could get to the sheriff at Bartow, two more stage stops away.

The lady that had captured Mossy Back's eye decided to go back with Spurgeon to the depot. She rode one of the other horses as they were taken back to the corral for the night to await the sheriff the next few days, for Spurgeon was sure he would come out this way.

The lady had only a small valise and it was tied on to the third horse and all went toward the Tanner store and depot. Spurgeon took the lady up to the house and told Maude Elsie that the lady would stay overnight.

"What is your name, child?" Maude Elsie asked.

"Savannah Ford," she told Maude Elsie. Then she spoke for the first time and said, "I couldn't go on with the stage because of the man that was hurt."

"Do you know who he is?" Maude Elsie asked with a suspicious tone in her voice.

"No . . . no maam. You see, I am a trained nurse and I, well, I just thought I could assist you here in the woods, you know with the primitive conditions and all," she stammered.

Maude Elsie looked at Savannah and said, "Well, you are right there; we do live in the woods and the ways are primitive, but I don't think this man will live through the night," then added, "We still have to figure how to get him in the house."

"Can you stretch a tent over the travois and just let it rest with one end on the edge of the porch?" Savannah asked, "Then I can tend him without the extra burden of hurting him more by placing him in a bed."

Soon the Indian litter was resting on the porch and a blazing fire was glowing on each side of the travois.

"What are the fires for?" Savannah asked.

"Skeeters," Spurgeon answered as he piled more wood by each fire. "If you all is gonna ten to em all night the skeeters'll bout eat yew live." He threw bits of cotton cloth in the fires and told Savannah to take some of the rags and use them for a smudge fire to smoke the mosquitoes and keep them away.

When daybreak came, ending the long night, Savannah had fallen asleep in her chair beside the man on the travois.

Spurgeon nudged her and she jumped up startled, "Ah didn't thot ah'd scare ya none but here's a cup o' coffee and Maude Elsie has breakfuss ready." He looked at the man then asked.

"How long is he bin daid?"

"He isn't or he wasn't when I . . . I guess I fell asleep . . . is he dead, now?" she asked.

"Ah'm fraid so look lack he tried to move some, that whut kilt him iffen he woulda kept still he . . . well anyhow he's daid. Com'on in and git breakfast ah'll plant em after we et." Spurgeon took Savannah by the arm and led her into the kitchen.

The smells in the kitchen were so pleasant that Savannah wanted just to sniff them up as though she was storing the aromas in her memory for life.

"Smells just divine," Savannah said to Maude Elsie.

"Well it aint nothin but ole country cookin and surly you've smelt that b'fo aint you?" Maude Elsie replied.

"Now just sit down an eat yore fill and you can stay the nights till the stage comes through again and . . ." Maude Elsie held up as Spurgeon came up to the kitchen door stamping his feet on the wooden porch.

"My land, Spurgeon, you really need ta not make so much noise while I'm tryin to talk to Savannah."

"Thank you, maam. I would like to go and rest some after I eat this wonderful breakfast you made for me," Savannah said.

Spurgeon looked at the beautiful young lady really for the first time. She had auburn hair and her complexion was like fresh cream. He swallowed and then sat down at his normal place at the table. The conversation was polite and sporadic until the dishes were clear and the second cup of coffee was in front of each one at the table.

"Whar ya frum missie?" Spurgeon asked, and Maude Elsie said, "tsk," then added "Spurgeon you know that her name is Savannah and so she must be from Savannah, Georgia."

"Naw, I don't know that, at aires tha reason I asked her," Spurgeon answered.

"Well actually I'm from Milledgeville, Georgia; I was named Savannah by my grandmother who was named Savannah too. So I carry the name on and am proud of that too because when she passed away the last thing she said was "Savannah," so my name is both largely proud and sad for me," Savannah said humbly.

Spurgeon drank down the last swallow of his coffee from the saucer, set the cup into the saucer and said, "I best be gittin out ta them horses what jist come in from the run."

THE LONG DAYS OF
HARD WORK

Maud Elsie went in to the pantry and retrieved a bar of home made lye soap she had made last Fall when they butchered the hogs. She thought for a minute then went back in and gathered a can of sausage that was canned at the same time. "We can have the sausage and greens with corn bread for supper," she mused as she sat the can on the kitchen table.

Spurgeon came to the door and asked if there were any words to be said over the man he had just buried? "I didn't know the feller but even though he be a robber, thar aught to be somethin said overn hissens grave."

"Well," Maude Elsie thought out loud, "we can maybe keep on and let the parson say something over his grave when he comes by here heading to church at Bent Penny this Sunday."

"At's a good idee, and then I can git on wid tha chores I gotta do this mawnin," Spurgeon said as he turned and walked toward the barn.

Savannah seemed to appear into the kitchen from out of no where, and as she spoke Maude Elsie jumped and said, "Oh my lands Savannah you just about skeert me out a ten years of my life_"

Savannah smiled her apology and took the bar of soap from Maude Elsies hand. "What do you plan to do with this?" she asked.

"Today's Monday aint it?" Maude Elsie said.

"Yes maam it is," Savannah said, "Then this must be wash day," she added.

There was almost ten cords of wood chopped and stacked beside the house and the wash pot was being fired with pieces from the cord, soon the water would be boiling for the first load of washing to be done that day.

Even though the shade of the ancient oaks lowered the tempature, sweat ran down Maude Elsie and Savannah's faces and soon their dresses were wet with the perspiration, their aprons were wet from wiping their faces, all caused by the unrelenting Florida summer sun and the heat from the fire under the wash pot.

Maude Elsie used a long stick to punch the wash around in the boiling water, with the same stick would plop the wash into the wash tub full of cold water to rinse. The wash was always rinsed twice, then wrung out as best they could, the clothes were hung on the clothes line to dry in the warm breeze of the Florida day.

As the clothes dried, Savannah took them from the clothes line and into the house to be ironed on the morrow.

Another hot humid new, Tuesday, met the pair as they heated the flat irons on the wood stove. When the iron got cooler it was replaced by another waiting on the hot, wood fired stove. The back porch was the coolest place they could find for this chore, and be out of the flies, and gnats.

Spurgeon stayed clear of the porch while the ironing was in progress. He would slip into the kitchen and make himself a sandwich of cold biscuit and left over sausage or bacon from breakfast, pour himself a cup of coffee, then back to the forge or the tack room to repair harnesses or re-shoe a horse before the next run.

The ironing was held up in time to begin the meal that would greet the folks on the stagecoach when it arrived at one o'clock; unless it was not on time which was usually the rule rather than the exception.

While they were waiting for the flat irons to heat on the stove, Maude Elsie and Savannah, picked almost a bushel of black eye peas and there was squash and greens cooked. A large ham had been brought from the smoke house and it was in the oven to roast along with sweet potatoes. Maude Elsie went to the pantry and put the canned sausage back on the shelf.

The stage was about an hour and a half late. The people were hungry, thirsty, tired and dusty; ready to be on solid ground, not to mention getting the dirt and dust out of their mouths and noses.

The cool sweet tea was the best drink in the house, as the folks drank, the food was hardly touched but the iced tea and cool water was completely consumed. The ice wagon had delivered fifty pounds of ice from the new ice plant in Bartow; the ice wagon came every other day and there was always the need for that fifty pounds of ice at the depot.

Mossy Back and Efrim had eaten and were out tending the teams that Spurgeon had readied for the next ten mile run.

Mossy Back called Spurgeon over to the side of the stagecoach and asked, "Is that purty lady still a gonna stay with yall some longer?"

"I guess so, she's been so much help to Maude Elsie, I don't know whut she'd do iffen she was ta went now," Spurgeon answered. Then asked, "Why you ask fer that no how Mossy?"

"They's a feller over ta Tamper what has lost hissen's be-trothed and now he done went and wont to give a reward fer to find that there fellers woman lady," Mossy Back answered.

Efrim had come up and was listening to the gossip spilled forth by Mossy and added,

"Yup he gonna give a hunert dollar gold fer where she's at, thin he'll come and fetch her I reccon."

"I guess mebbe miz Savannah should oughta know bout him and hissens ree-ward iffen she be the one wut he done been a lookin' fer," Spurgeon said, and shook his head as he walked away from the other two men.

After the stage had pulled away and the dust had again settled around the stage stop the business of the day continued.

The irons were again hot and Maude Elsie and Savannah were on the back porch laboring over the hot irons, and starched clothes.

Spurgeon walked up and sat on the rail near the porch steps and pondered for a few minutes, then just blurted out, "Savannah, you got a beau?" Then he stuttered, "I . . . I ah . . . Mmmm . . . uh . . . Ole Mossy Back done said thar war a feller over to Tamper whuts a wont's ta give a bounty of a hunert dollar gold fer the return of hissen be-trothed; Savannah is youens her?"

Savannah set her iron on the end of the ironing board where a large can lid was sitting, to keep the hot iron from scorching the pad. She looked at Maude Elsie and tears welled up in her eyes.

Maude Elsie sat her iron on the plate of the stove and went and put her arm around Savannah, and asked, "What's it all about child?" Then she started to escort Savannah to the kitchen where they all three sat at the table in silence, waiting for Savannah to react.

At long last Savannah spoke, "Yes, his name is Dirk Richards and he's been after me for a long, long time to marry him, but I just don't love the man. We've known each other since we were small children. His parents moved in next door to us and we went to school together. He felt as though he owned me and after college he really went over the line. I moved to Tampa to get away from him, now he has followed me here too. I just don't know where I am going to turn now," she started weeping and dabbed her eyes with her apron.

"Fust off, youens is a gonna stay rat cheer and make this ole stage depot yore home wid us and iffen inny body comes a snoopin round heer he gonna git whut fer," Spurgeon said as he rose from the table to get all a glass of tea.

"Oh Spurgeon, hush, and let the child finish tellin us about this here feller," Maude Elsie scolded her husband. Then looked at Savannah and said, "go on honey and tell us what you want to do about this man."

"I just don't want to have anything to do with him, and if I can't get away from him; I don't know what I will do," Savannah sobbed.

Maude Elsie and Spurgeon both reached out and touched Savannah on the arm and as they stroked her they assured her that nothing would happen to her as long as she stayed in the depot with them.

As they were consoling Savannah a horse and buggy drove up in the yard. A young well dressed, well built man got down and stepped up on the porch to the kitchen and knocked on the door.

Savannah ran to her bedroom and closed the door.

Spurgeon went to the door and looked at the man up and down then asked, "whut choo wont?"

"I am Dirk Richards and I was told that a young lady answering to the description of my fiancee is staying here, and if she is here I just want to speak to her for a few minutes. Is she indeed here, sir?"

"Whut choo wont ta say to her if she be here, mister?" Spurgeon squinted as he questioned.

"Sir, that would be between Miss Savannah and me now, wouldn't it?" the young man retorted.

"Now yew jist listen ta me you young . . ." Spurgeon stopped as Maude Elsie came to the door and stood beside him.

"Wont you come in and have a glass of tea with Spurgeon and myself?" Maude Elsie said to head off the impending confrontation that was sure to happen if Spurgeon kept talking.

"Uh . . . no maam, I just want to know if Savannah is here of not," the young man answered.

Maude Elsie then said that Savannah had indeed been there but wasn't present just now, and if he had no other business then she needed to continue with her ironing.

The man turned and climbed up into the buggy, whipped the horses mercilessly as they churned up the dust in the dooryard, so much so that it obscured the buggy from their sight as they watched it head back west toward Tampa.

Savannah came out of her room when she heard the buggy leave and said, "I hope he's gone for good. Now Miz Maude Elsie we better get this ironing done and put an end to this long hot day of hard work."

A SHOT FROM THE SCRUB

Mossy Back reined the horses up in front of the depot and he and Efrim climbed down. Efrim went on unhooking the team as Mossy opened the stagecoach door to let the passengers alight as he shouted, "All out we gonna be heer thuty minutes, the ladies use the privy and you men use the scrub. Wash up around back by tha pump and don't forget ta leave water ta prime tha pump."

Just as Efrim was closing the gate to the corral where he had pent the old team, and was walking toward the stage a shot rang out and hit the dirt between his legs. He didn't miss a beat but ran behind the stagecoach and looked toward the scrub where the shot came from.

Spurgeon had run to the house and grabbed his Colt and Winchester. He eased out the back door and into the scrub. He was quiet as an Indian. He crept within shooting distance of where the shot had come from. He heard what sounded like a rifle lever being worked, stepped behind a tree then spoke.

"Yew jist about hit the stage driver and now youens better step out and let me see who is a shootin up my stage depot," Spurgeon shouted.

Another shot rang out and the bullet hit the tree just in front of Spurgeon.

Spurgeon took aim and fired at the smoke coming out of a palmetto patch a few yards in front of him. The palmettoes shook as though someone was running from that patch, then only stillness.

Spurgeon shouted again and said, "Yew wont sum more ov this here Winchester?"

Silence.

Spurgeon moved from tree to tree always keeping the shooters lair in sight. Soon he was standing in the palmetto patch the shooter was using, where he found a lot of blood. He tracked it as he had deer he had shot that didn't drop on the spot. Soon about ten yards from the patch he found the man who he knew as Dirk Richards, lying on the ground looking up at the sky with sightless eyes and a 30-30 bullet hole through his chest.

Tom Walker and Cliff Teague were on their way to Bartow now the County Seat of Polk County. They had stopped in at the stage depot for some lunch. They kept all the passengers from the stagecoach down as low as possible inside the house while the shooting was happening. They watched as Spurgeon walked across the dooryard with the body draped over his shoulder, the Winchester in his left hand and the Colt still stuck in his belt.

Spurgeon let the body drop on to the white sand on the front yard and shouted for Maude Elsie, but she was already coming through the screen door to the porch.

"Who is it, Spurgeon?" Maude Elsie asked.

"Hit be that thar feller whot was heer t'other day and wanted ta talk ta Savannah. He don't wont ta talk ta her no more," Spurgeon spoke loudly so that Savannah would hear but not come out of the house to see the dead body of her suitor.

The next stagecoach from Bent Penny to Bartow would spread the news with a news paper, "A fellow named Dirk Richards, was killed in a gunfight and is dead and buried at the Tanner stage depot. Anyone who wishes to claim the body will have to contact the local undertaker," read the article in the Polk County Democrat. The newspaper carried the story and it created curiosity in a lot of folks in Ft. Cummins, Bartow and surrounding homesteads so they rode the stagecoach, horses, buggies and on foot to the Tanner stage depot just to see where the "gun fight" happened.

Spurgeon and Maude Elsie feared the influx of a large group of people at one time would be more than the ladies and cow hands at the settlement would be able to handle. It was a small settlement, just the stage stop and general store, but the resourcefulness of Maude Elsie and Spurgeon there was a fine spread on the picnic style tables under the oaks where the washing had been done only last Monday.

Spurgeon put a price on the meal of forty-five cents and the menu was hand printed by Savannah's stylish hand with pen and ink:" Roasted beef, or Baked ham, mashed potatoes, or baked sweet potatoes, black-eyed peas, turnip greens with turnips, fresh bread or cornbread, hot coffee, iced tea, ice water or lemonade, and for dessert lemon pie or honey cakes."

The influx of people was so that when Mary Sykes-Remmick from the Bent Penny Ranch heard that Maude Elsie had so much work trying to keep the people fed and then placed to keep from over loading the grounds around the store and depot. She sent Willie Mae and John Henry Luke, Tom Walker, his Seminole Indian wife, Orange Blossom, along with Cliff Teague to assist with the chores caused by the horde of people coming by stagecoach and then returning on the special stage Spurgeon had to bring on line for a return stage to Ft. Cummins and Bartow.

In short order John Henry had fire wood stacked for the kitchen and the guests were charged fifty cents for enough wood to last the night ; many of the people were camping there on the settlement grounds.

Cliff and Tom were dragging in trees to be cut up for wood and cypress saplings for poles for the campers to make tepees to sleep in.

A wagon with what looked like a small house with ginger bread trim came up with four smart shiny black horses pulling it and as it happened the only place for it to park was across the dirt road that the stagecoaches used to go and come. The driver got down and let the side and rear stages down exposing a pipe organ like contraption which after a fire was lit in the boiler and the steam was up the driver of the show wagon sat at a key board and started to play the calliope. With the stream of music coming from the wagon the horses, mules, dogs and cats around the house began to look for a safer place to be.

Spurgeon who seldom gets too excited about anything took off in a run for the offending wagon, grabbed the musician by the collar and through him to the ground.

"What choo tryin ta do skeer them dumb animals plum to death? You done jis 'bout caused a stampede from tha corral, now you cut out that cat-a-wallerin and git out o' heer and ah means now," Spurgeon nearly screamed at the man.

The man got up off the ground and plead, "My good man if I may, I simply want to add a bit of music and perhaps a little thespian activity to this fine festival."

'Festival is it?" Spurgeon questioned, then asked, "you got a fiddle?"

The man answered, "Yes sir I do and several other instruments too."

Spurgeon ordered as he walked away, "Bring em ta tha front porch and set up thar."

Soon there was an entire orchestra on the porch playing tune after tune, as the people, some of whom had their own instruments began to play while others chose partners and began to dance on the white sand in front of the depot.

Meanwhile Maude Elsie and Mary were watching over the buffet as Willie Mae and Orange Blossom were passing among the diners offering refills of iced tea or ice water or lemonade.

The crowd was enjoying the music and the dancing. Two malcontents who were settlers back in the scrub, had a liquor still and began selling the moonshine to the people around the scrub who would buy the brew from them. They were circulating through the crowd selling drinks from the jugs and when one would get empty they had others near by and soon there was enough of the shine running through the blood of a few men in the crowd that a fight broke out near the wagon of the music man, just as it spread across the road to the yard where the picnic tables were, Spurgeon stepped out on the front porch and went to the front steps. He stuck the barrel of the shot gun in the air and both barrels went at once. The quiet that settled over the crowd immediately was almost deafening.

"Now you all whuts a fighten out cheer you stop and I mean stop rat now, or the next two shots you hear will be a headen fer yur guts. Now you drunks pack it up and leave or go to bed and when you wake up you leave my property, Now Git_ And if any of you all puke you git a shovel and clean it up. I aint gonna have my yard smellin lack no barroom floor," Spurgeon said as he reloaded the twelve guage.

The quiet stayed the crowd and the musicians packed up the instruments and were heading for their space for the night.

The party had broken up and for the first time that day Maude Elsie had a minute to speak to Mary and Willie Mae and to go to Blossom and hug her for her help in feeding the two hundred or so people, who had come to see where a man was killed.

The morning would be brutal as they were behind the schedule by two days as the next day would be Wednesday and the washing and ironing was not done and the baking was to be done that very next day.

Mary, Blossom and Willie Mae stayed for two more days and helped the Tanners get things back in order and on schedule.

As Friday rolled around the wagon with the house still stood in front of the depot but the sides were folded and ready to roll but there was no sign of the musician driver. Spurgeon went to the wagon several times and looked inside but there was no one in the wagon. The horses were still in the corral and eating their heads off. That was something that Spurgeon was not going to have. He figured that if the horses were going to eat they were going to work. So the next day when Mossy and Efrim stopped at the depot, four black shiny horses were pulling second behind a pair of well seasoned horses that would teach the new pairs to hump through the Florida sand to and from Tampa and Ft. Cummins.

THE FIDDLER RETURNS

Several days had passed when Maude Elsie noticed a small camp fire glowing at the rear of the wagon with the calliope. She sent Spurgeon out to check on the wagon and to see if the musician had returned.

He had indeed, and to say that he was in a bad way is a grand understatement, for the man looked as though he had not slept or eaten in as long a time as he had been away from his wagon. He was sitting on the edge of his wagon seat in his underwear looking at the fire.

"Whut choo been a doin fer tha las few days mister . . . You got a name musician?" Spurgeon asked.

"Yes sir, my name is Professor Tillman Clark, I have played for Doctors, Lawyers, Bankers, Indian Chiefs and the Crown Heads of the British Isles, but sir never . . . no, never have I played at such a soiree as was before me Tuesday last. Why sir your festival was to end all festivals and I think, no, I shall sell everything I own and rest right here if there is no objection from you and the lady of this villa. I could, at least throw my spectacles in the ash bin for now I have seen everything worthy of seeing or being seen," the musician exclaimed with a deep British accent.

"Huh?" Spurgeon seemed to have heard every word the man said but did not comprehend any part of it after, "Indian Chief."

"Need I repeat myself kind sir?" the musician asked as though he were restating the entire question again.

"No . . . you just answer me one thang, where is you been fer tha las three day Mr. Professor?" Spurgeon asked.

"Two men with the makings of demon rum whisked me away like I

18

was on a magic carpet ride. You see sir I have a failing for the spirits and what they were selling from the voluminous demijon was more than I could refuse, and I just followed those men to their lair to find a limitless supply of their elixir . . . and lo I was taken for all that I owned but for my hapless little mobile abode here and now even my beautiful steeds are missing. For they took my hat, my clothes, my boots and my rings . . . what have I to show for it. Nothing even my beautiful steeds are gone now," the man stated with grief in his tone of voice.

"Your horses aint stole, Mr. Professor, they's jist working fer a livin' see they was in my livery eaten and a eaten so I done put them pullers of youren ta work a pullin my stagecoach to Tamper, they is due back come Sunday," Spurgeon told the professor. Then added, "Now you come on over ta tha sto an we'uns will give you some clothes to wear ta work in till you has paid for the feed and grain them horses et fer three day afore I hitched em ta tha stage ta work."

"Maude Elsie, that music man aint run off he jist follert tha Doollie boys ta home and they robbed him o every thin but his'ns BVD's," Spurgeon told Maude Elsie as he brought the hapless man into the store to outfit him.

The man was as good as his word and worked hard and long hours for Spurgeon but he ate like a starving hound at each meal, making Spurgeon think other thoughts about keeping him for very long. Maybe he should cut his losses and let the man hitch up his team and leave less he have to put in more provisions. The black horses did make good pullers and he used them as much as he could to work some of the three days of feed and grain given to the horses in his livery.

Savannah had enjoyed the professor with his expounding tales of his exploits around the world and lately in the United States and his adventures into Florida. Almost every night now she has been singing to the melodious tunes he played on his violin or cello. Since he had been in the United States he had picked up the guitar and the banjo and was very good at them, his talents were expanding and his warmth for the Tanners and Savannah was deepening all the while. Though he was near twice the age of Savannah he was under her spell and felt that if he did not hold her in his arms he would surely die, and if he did he would likely swoon away from holding such a beautiful young lady as she. It was not to be for he knew that he was too old and not well enough in health nor finances to even think of such thoughts.

After about two weeks the household awoke and Spurgeon went out to wake up the professor in his wagon to find that in the dark of the night he had pulled out and left a note with two gold rings tied up with a lavender ribbon as a gift to Maude Elsie and Savannah. To Spurgeon he left a pearl handle knife in a leather sheath with gold and silver studs on the case, a wonderful gift and thoughtful too.

Some weeks later Spurgeon and his cow hands were combing the scrub below Blue Forrest as he came to a clear sand bottom pond he heard cows lowing and bellowing as if they were in pain, he kept riding his little marsh tackie toward the sound and found the cattle in a place where cows would not ordinarily gather, as bunch critters like this. He looked and looked for any sign of a man or men having driven the cattle into this type of setting but saw no sign of horses or foot prints that would indicate that the Indians around these parts were responsible for the bunch critters here.

He cracked his whip and sent the catch dogs in after the cattle to drive them from the ring of palmettoes that had kept them hemmed in until they were about to die of thirst. The cows went strait for the water and drank and drank until Spurgeon had to sic the dogs on them and chase them out of the water lest they founder from too much water at once. This was the first time he thought to count the cows in the bunch and as he was counting he heard hoof beats coming through the scrub as they followed the Indian trail to the pond just as he had one hour before.

The horses came into the clearing where the pond was and the dozen head of cattle that Spurgeon had rescued from the palmettoes. But before they could see him he eased his tackie into the pine and oak thicket to be all but invisible to the one coming into the pond clearing. The cows spooked and shied away from the on coming horses until they stopped in the clearing too.

Spurgeon recognized the Doolie brothers Luke the oldest and Cleotis the younger and both as mean as snakes when they were sober but drunk they were not to be dealt with at all. This is the reason they stayed in the scrub most of the time, and when they went to town it was to trade moonshine for staples, ammunition, and supplies to make more moonshine. The last place that Spurgeon wanted to be was by himself in the scrub with the Doolie brothers. So he loosened the tie down on the hammer of his colt peace maker and eased a round in the chamber of his new Henry rifle chambered in the.45 caliber long colt as his pistol was, then he waited.

"Now who you rec'n turnt these here bunch critters a loose from them palmetters?" Luke almost shouted at Cleotis.

"I don't know Luke I warn't here when hit happent, I wuz wit choo I thank," Cleotis answered.

"Well we best git em back in ta tha palmetters so's we kin git some more to trade in town nex week," Luke told his brother.

Spurgeon kept quiet in the thicket until they had bunched the cattle up again and drove them back into the palmettoes. Then they rode off at a gallop as they had come in. Spurgeon waited until he could not hear the two men anymore and then he eased out of the thicket and wiped the sweat off his brow with his kerchief. He drifted back south until he met with his hands and asked if any of them had heard or seen the Doolies. They had not so he figured that they had gone back to their house near the pond in the scrub. And as night fell on them they came to the place where the bunch critters were and drove them from the palmettoes. They stopped for the night at a hammock east of the blue forest lake and built a fire the cattle were content to graze on the lush grass around the edge of the lake and did not wander too far in the night.

Morning brought the smell of bacon cooking and coffee boiling as the men got ready to meet the day and after they had eaten and the cook had cleaned up the men were saddling their horses when a shot rang out of the forest and through the hat of one of the cow hands. He dropped to the ground, and the cook threw water on the campfire at the same time. All were ready when another bullet whizzed through the camp, then the sound of the bullet being fired which meant the assailant was some distance away when the second round was sent toward the camp. Spurgeon held up two fingers meaning there were two firing at them and one was further into the forest than the other. Spurgeon looked for something that would be better protection than the chuck wagon wheel and spotted the cypress tree near the water of the lake just four feet from where he was squatting. He dashed to the tree as a bullet hit the ground behind him. That time he saw the flash in the early morning darkness and fired at the spot and heard the man let an oath that would make a barkeep blush. Then the man screamed into the scrub, "Luke . . . Luke, I done been shot, he done shot me and I caint see to . . . Luke . . ." Then silence. The next shot came from almost the right hand as though the other man had been running through the scrub when his brother was shot. There was a volley of fire from the cowboys and the scrub fell silent again. When the sun was up they all went to see where they had shot and found Luke sitting on a stump leaning against a pine tree with three holes in his chest. His rifle between his legs with the muzzle in the dirt and his pistol still in his belt. They looked for Cleotis and found him where he had fallen in the scrub with a single hole in his left chest. His rifle was still in his hands and his pistol on the ground beside him. His toothless smile and sightless eyes were looking into the pines above him.

Spurgeon decided to go by their house and bury the two men on their homestead that actually belonged to the Bent Penny Ranch. When the house was in site there in the front yard was the Professor's wagon the horses were in the corral and the tack was in the wagon but no sign of the professor. Every one hunted for the man and soon his body was found near the back of the swamp where he was recognized by the clothes that Spurgeon had given him. There was no sign of how he died for there was just a skeleton in the clothes. Spurgeon spoke, "He probably drunk his self to death cause he done said he liked wiskey."

They hitched up the horses to the wagon and drove it to the depot and parked it across the road from the depot and put the horses in the pulling lot after they were fed, watered and brushed.

ALONG THE BENT PENNY TRACE

The Tanner stagecoach was running about as usual, one hour late. Just as the coach turned a long turn around a bay head Mossy Back pulled on the reins and Efrim set the brakes on the coach. The people in the coach yelled their displeasure at the rough treatment but soon were calmed when Mossy and Efrim both yelled at the same time to brace for a hard bump.

A pine sapling and a large cypress log had fallen across the clay road and in spite of the haul-back on the lines the driver and Efrim knew that the coach was going to hit the largest log and if they were lucky the coach wouldn't turn over on its side. The coach hit the stump with the right front wheel first, the wheel turned to the right and quickly following the rear wheel hit the stump. The left front steel tire went singing its bell like tune past the horses and into the swamp. The coach lunged over the stump with the rear and much larger diameter wheel then settled back on to the clay road. Mossy was hauling the lines for all he was worth when the shock of the rear humped the coach a good three feet in the air then settled down on the clay. The horses were skidding along on the clay trying to stop but the momentum of the coach and their large bodies fell to inertia and slid some twenty feet before resting on the back of the horses back legs then springing up and regaining balance until the still rolling stage pushed the skidding horses another four or five feet.

Efrim was jarred loose from his perch on the right hand side of the box, had he not flung the shot gun away and grabbed on to the bucking brace handles of the seat would have been thrown to the ground. As it was he was hanging over the side of the coach only inches from having his left leg entangled in the front wheel now turned ninety degrees from the way of travel.

Mossy was in worse shape since he was hauling back on the lines and when the coach hit the log he was thrown on to the back of the right rear horse. He grabbed the collar and held on for dear life as the horses slid to a stop.

When all the commotion had ended Efrim let himself down to the ground, ran to the side of the coach and jerked the door open. Mossy was also on the ground and snatched the right-hand door open. There was a tangle of legs arms on the floor between the seats as Mossy and Efrim began to separate the tangle of humanity there in the bowels of that coach. The first out was a man that had the knees of one of the lady passengers and both came out of the coach head to foot and she landed on him in the clay. Then next, and next, until all were out of the coach and in different ways of regaining their footing there beside the stagecoach.

As soon as it was determined that no one was seriously injured but had scratches and bruises, the driver and his shotgun guard walked around the stagecoach to survey the damage. The right front wheel had lost the steel tire and thus had collapsed onto the broken spokes. Mossy asked Efrim to unhitch the lead horse and ride the two miles back to the Bent Penny Ranch and get another wheel, or get the black smith to see what could be done to repair the broken coach.

In about four hours the black smith pulled up with a smaller wheel then looked at the kingpin under the front axle it was bent like a horse shoe but the smithy had guessed that the pin would be of little or no use after the wheel had turned the way Efrim had described.

Old Will Henry, who was employed with the David Crocket Pearce Engineering Co., and drove the survey wagon, also maintained the equipment and helped manage the salt business at the Bent Penny Ranch. Old Will Henry came up driving the school wagon, and assisted the women on to the wagon, the men crawled up on the wagon and waited for Will Henry to get it moving back toward the Bent Penny Ranch.

After another two hour ride the wagon pulled up to the door of the dining hall and as they alighted to the ground walked into the long hall where Mary Sykes-Remmick directed them to sit near the kitchen and soon were served a very welcomed meal. The dining hall was abuzz with the stories about the mishap and soon the people from the stage found how tired they were, Mary had blossom and Willie Mae set up the cots in the dining hall for the ladies and the men went to the bunk house where extra cots were set up for them.

The rooster crowed, as dawn broke across the compound and the men were surprised to find the cowhands were already up and gone. They dragged their sore bodies into the dining hall and sat with the women who were also up and moving slow as they were sore in their muscles too.

During the night the stagecoach had limped onto the compound and the clang, clang of the smithy's hammer rang the tune of repair. Around noon the stagecoach was proclaimed fit and the passengers again loaded onto the conveyance for the balance of their trip to Tampa.

As they arrived at the same curve they all noticed that the logs were pulled from the road and there was little else to mar the final destination to the Tanners depot.

As the stagecoach pulled up to the front of the depot Maude Elsie and Spurgeon were in the sunshine assisting the passengers down from the coach. There was little talk until Spurgeon asked for the names and addresses of each passenger for the records and to file the insurance on the wheel. One man asked to stay at the depot until the stage ran again in two days. Spurgeon put him up in the bunk house with the cowhands for the two nights.

Maude Elsie called the hands to supper and watched as the man came in and found himself a place at the long table. After the blessing was asked the men began to eat and paid little attention to Savannah as she served the men or kept the glasses filled. The new man at the table noticed her. Savannah served him several time and the other men began to notice and started teasing her about her service to the man. After the meal the men were sitting on the front porch of the general store, swapping stories when one of them ask the man what his name was.

"Hayman, Claude Hayman, I am on my way to Tampa to catch a steamboat to New Orleans. I have to see a relative there who is dividing the family belongings to empty the old house and sell the property," he answered and added, "I would rather stay here in Florida and work as a railroad telegrapher though."

Maude Elsie, Spurgeon and Savannah walked onto the porch where the evening was cool and the smudge-pots were putting out the smoke from cotton cloth burning to keep the mosquitos away. The full moon was rising the shadows were long and as it climbed in the sky Claude looked up to see Savannah watching him as he talked to the other men.

Claude became uncomfortable as he felt Savannah's eyes on him and moved nervously as the conversation went on and soon came back to the mishap on the trail the day before. Spurgeon told them, "I tried to pay for the smithy and the wheelwright's time and for the meals they served, but Earl Ray or Jeremiah would not let me pay for anything but the wheel, you just cant beat good neighbors like those at the Bent Penny Ranch."

Spurgeon was awakened at three in the morning by the sounds of a rig of some sort pulling up in the front of the depot and store. He slipped into his pants and boots, then easing the colt pistol into his waist, stepped into the depot waiting room. The full moon shown bright and the shadows in the road were clear enough but Spurgeon did not recognize either of the men as they walked up to the depot door.

As they entered the unlocked door, Spurgeon struck a match and lit the coal oil lamp on the ticket cage desk. At that point he recognized the big man on his left was Sheriff Stanley Melrose, who wanted to be called Mel. The other person was handcuffed and had leg shackles on that prevented him from making steps beyond a little greater than the length of his other foot. "You couldn't run if the world was afar," Spurgeon muttered to himself. Then said, "Whut kin ah do fer ye shuruff, a comin here at this time o mawnin?"

"I have this prisoner I picked up at the Ft. Cummins railroad depot, I been travelin most all night now to get to Bartow by dawn but I aint gonna make it, so we pulled in here to get a cup of Maude Elsie's coffee and to use the privy," the sheriff said in an apologetic manor.

"Where did y'all come frum, they aint got no scrub where you come frum why in the dangies do ye need ta use ourn privy for? We use that thar fer the wimen whut rides tha stage and fer Maude Elsie and Savannah here, why I aint never heered nuthin so . . ." The sheriff interrupted Spurgeon's tirade and said, "This here feller is a female women and she done helt up tha bank in Kissimmee, we shot her'n husband or whut ever he was to her, but he daid anyhow and now we gonna have a trial at Bartow this very day and they prob'ly gonna hang her," then added, "Yall comin ta tha trial?"

Spurgeon answered under his breath, "Wouldn't go ta see no female wimen hang, jist lack ah wont go ta tha . . ." Maude Elsie and Savanah walked into the depot after hearing the voices and the sheriff asked her if she would accompany the prisoner into the privy and make sure she didn't escape.

Maude Elsie obliged the sheriff and waited inside the privy for the prisoner to do her business then as they exited the sheriff replaced the handcuffs.

"Mel, aint you gonna let her wash up before she eats after using the privy?" Maude Elsie asked the sheriff.

"Yessum, she don't need them cuffs off fer that though tha water wont hurt um none," Mel replied.

While Maude Elsie was attending the prisoner, Savannah had started the coffee then had the stove hot enough to make breakfast; even though it was still almost an hour before the regular getting up time the hands started coming in and sitting around the dining room to see what the fuss was all about.

The sheriff ate a hearty meal but the woman prisoner hardly had more than a few sips of the coffee Savannah sat before her.

Savanah looked into the woman's eyes as she placed her food before her, and noticed a look of pleading or some type of signal that can only be passed from woman to woman. While they were sitting and eating Savannah asked Maude Elsie what was the young woman doing all trussed up like she was? Then Maude Elsie asked the sheriff what she had done and he repeated what he had told Spurgeon soon after they drove up.

"Mel, you know that you are looking at hanging two people don't you?" Maude Elsie asked the sheriff.

The sheriff looked as though she had hit him with a board, "What choo mean, Maude Elsie, who be tha tuther'n?"

Maude Elsie looked at the young woman and said, "This young woman and her baby, you see she is about three months pregnant. I could tell the way she acted when she went to the toilet, and having had three sons of my own I can tell when a cat, cow, horse or a woman is going to have a baby."

Spurgeon looked at Maude Elsie, then at the young woman, then at

Savannah as though the latter would explain what his wife was talking about. "Maude Elsie don't you meddle in the law's business now you jist let it drop." Spurgeon almost shouted at Maude Elsie. Then he turned to one of the cowhands and told him to go see to the peace officer's rig and horses that they were watered and fed if needed.

The hand whispered something in the ear of his buddy next to him then picked up and left the room.

"I caint hang no woman who is a gonna have a baby," Mel sputtered then went to the kitchen and came back with the coffee pot and poured himself and the young woman another cup of coffee. He wheezed as he asked the prisoner, "Why'ent you told me this a fore ah done put on them irons?"

The young woman prisoner looked at Mel and with tears in her eyes sobbed, "You didn't give me even a minute with my husband, and you surely wouldn't listen to what I was trying to tell you at the depot," then she wiped her eyes on her sleeve and looked around the room.

"You all look at me and see the dangerously fierce, criminal that sheriff Mel has captured and ready to hang. Now Sheriff you can take this as you will, but I had no idea that Russell was going to try to hold up the bank in Kissimmee. He told me he was going to draw out enough to pay our food bill at the general store there. I was waiting out side and holding the team when I heard the shooting inside the bank.

It was like my heart went out of me as I realized what Russell had really gone into the bank for now. When Russell lost his job at the sawmill he tried to drive cows from the scrub and the first that he rounded up were stolen that night by rustlers and when he went to ask Mr. Bodow at the general store for a little more credit he was turned down and that's when Russell began to change.

He tried the railroad but since he did not get a letter of recommendation from the sawmill the railroad wouldn't hire him, and Russell began to panic. Yesterday afternoon he told me he was going to take me to Sanford, where he thought he could get a job as a deck hand on a steamboat. But I know now that was just to get me to go with him to hold up the bank. If I had known what was on his mind I would have whipped up those horses and we would not have stopped until we got to Sanford or the horses dropped over dead from running."

The young woman was openly sobbing now as she let her grief and her frustration go at the same moment. Maude Elsie and Savannah moved to her side and put their arms around her as she continued to sob now into the warm apron worn by Maude Elsie.

A great deal had happened today along the Bent Penny Trace.

A SPEEDY TRIAL

"The court will come to order, the honorable Taxdale Lightman, of the fifth circuit of the state of Florida presiding; ye all be seated or be heard."

The court clerk rapped the gavel on the desk and the courtroom fell silent. The judge entered the packed courtroom with a twirl of his robe and a flourish as he sat down into his overstuffed chair. He rapped his gavel and called the two opposing lawyers to the bench. "Now if either of you try to make a circus out of my courtroom I will find you in contempt and you will be spending the next ninety days in the county jail at hard labor plus a one hundred dollar fine for each or every offense. Is this perfectly clear, gentlemen."

"Yessir," was the dual answer from the two men as they spoke at the same time.

"Mr. Prosecutor you may begin your case," The Judge stated as he noisily closed the cover to his solid gold watch.

The courtroom was hot from the weather, and so many people that there were several recesses as people had to be carried out of the room because of the heat and the lack of circulation of air in the room. Straw fans were in evidence throughout the courtroom and the water on the judges bench and the opposing attorneys table these pitchers were consumed and had to be refilled at each recess. Open windows added little to the ventilation of the courtroom yet an occasional breath of wind seldom went further into the room than the window sill. The courtroom and all the people wished for a rain storm to cool the air throughout the town and especially the courtroom.

By early afternoon the prosecutor had rested and the defense council took over the trial; an uproar went up at his opening statement. When he looked at the jury and asked, "Are you willing to hang this young woman knowing that she is going to have a baby? And in Mrs. Maude Elsie Tanner's words you will be hanging her and her baby too? Are you willing to do that and still live with yourselves and do you think that your wives will be very cordial when you get home tonight? I don't think so and I hope they won't . . ."

"Objection_" the prosecutor shouted.

"Over ruled," the judge retorted.

"Exception_" the prosecutor shouted.

"Mr. Prosecutor you are in contempt of court, one hundred dollars and if it happens again you will get the ninety days I promised you earlier today. Now continue with your defense sir." The judge silenced the lawyer and smiled at the jury.

"Gentlemen of the jury this young lady is the victim here not the bank in Kissimmee as it has its money. This young lady was holding the horses in front of the bank where she thought her husband was transacting legitimate business in the bank, and knew nothing about the robbery until she heard the shots, as her husband was being mortally wounded. For in her words, "If I had known that he was going to do something like that I would have whipped up those horses and run them until we got to Sanford or they dropped dead from running." Now look at this lady who is accused of this crime. Can you distinguish from her demeanor where her criminal action came from? I certainly think not. Now I ask you Judge that you dismiss all charges against this young woman and let her get on with her life as best that she can. Thank You."

The Judge called a ten minute recess, when he came back into the courtroom he stated, "A wrong has been done to this young lady and I will not be a part of it. Case dismissed."

The courtroom exploded with applause and whistles, hog calls and even some cowboy cracked his whip.

People wondered as they filed out of the courtroom what was the young lady going to do with her life now that she had no husband and no place to live. But that was hardly a question as Maude Elsie and Spurgeon

Tanner, along with Savannah, loaded up in the wagon and lit out for the Tanner Stage Depot and General Store on the Bent Penny Trace.

They drove all day and into the next morning till around two a. m, the single wagon and two hands on horse back alit in front of the depot. The two hands helped unload the wagon then turned it around and parked it beside the barn. The men led the horses into the barn, curried them, fed them and put them into the corral. The men then went to the depot and each got a tin cup of coffee and Spurgeon dumped a jigger or two of his "shine" into the cups then sent the men to the bunkhouse to finish the coffee and the night.

The rooster crowed and clucked along the yellow pine split rail fence, then flapped his wings and crowed again.

"Awright . . . awright old man. Some day I'm agonna have you fer dinner. Your tough hide will go good with dumplins." Spurgeon spoke the threats to the rooster even though he knew the old bird was the best alarm clock on the place. He muttered to himself and anyone else who would listen, or could hear and understand what he was muttering about. Spurgeon pulled on his britches and shirt then thrust his elbows through the suspender straps, stretched, yawned and finally pulled on his boots and stood up to greet the morning.

Maude Elsie had been up the better part of two hours. The stove was hot and the coffee was boiling. The eggs had been gathered by Savannah, the lady from the trial began to fix breakfast for the folks at the depot.

"Honey, I don't know what your name is, we've been calling you the lady all the time, we heard that your late husband was named Russell, but we haven't heard what you are called,"

Maude Elsie spoke up and asked the lady.

"I'm Nadine Workman. My maiden name was Troute, like the fish but with an "e" at the end. Russell and I have been married only a year and eight months. We had built a small cabin out near the Davenport Still and sawmill. That's where he used to work for the German fellow Hans Nuddelman. We were buying five acres at the time from the land office in Kissimmee and doing fair when Mr. Nuddelman had to shut down the still and sawmill. We weren't the only ones who were in financial trouble, but Russell had said that we had money in the bank and not to worry. He would find a job but in the meantime he wanted to round up some scrub cows and when he got enough to sell he would drive them to the Bent Penny and let Mr. Coxin or Mr. Remmick take care of them. But that night the rustlers came and got all sixteen head of our cows.

I hate that place and I will go back there someday and burn it to the ground with everything in it. I just simply hate that place now." Nadine started to cry again and wept openly as Maude Elsie made her way to Nadine and put her arms around her to comfort her.

Savannah and Spurgeon finish putting on the breakfast while Maude Elsie consoled Nadine who wouldn't stop sobbing.

Nadine stood up, and with a scream, sank to the floor, Spurgeon scooped her up in his arms and took her to the room where she had slept that night before.

"Nadine's been asleepin almost two day now. Yall thank we'uns might oughta go fetch tha doc over ta Bartow now, you thank Maude Elsie," Spurgeon asked, then turned to look at her again.

"Naw, come on Savannah we are going to wake her up and end her shock at the same time," Maude Elsie said as she turned and followed Savannah into the ladies bedroom.

They took off her clothes and wrapped her in a sheet then took her to the wash tubs and placed her in the tub with her head and legs sticking out of the old wooden tub. Maude Elsie started pumping water into the tub and soon the cold water was nearly running over the brim of the tub, when, Nadine thrashed out as though someone was trying to hurt her. Then she opened her eyes and saw that she was in a cold bath and said, "I'm sorry, maam and I don't know what came over me. I just don't know."

"You was in shock. Honey, your poor little body had stood just all it could stand and you went into shock," Maude Elsie told Nadine. And with Savannah's help they lifted her out of the tub and walked her back into the house to get dressed.

Nadine's small four foot frame fitted her spirit well as she was like a little pixie and everything she touched turned out nearly perfect. She was the biggest help in the kitchen, where she could cook like a professional chef. The men liked her pancakes and some new things called a waffle. Spurgeon sent off to the mail order company for a special waffle making machine that fit over the stove eye and the waffle could be turned over and bake on the other side. She made them to taste like honey, cinnamon and smoked bacon. And as each one was served she dusted it with ten-x powdered sugar. Nadine did all of these little flourishes to make the meal look better on the plate and taste good too. She really threw herself into the meals she served. Soon, people were coming again just to eat the nearest thing to a gourmet meal that could be found in any scrub depot in the land.

It was several months before Nadine decided that she should go and close out the cabin, get what money she could back out of the land. Maybe the land office would buy the land back from her she thought as she drove the buggy to Davenport and the homestead.

When she arrived she found that a family of squatters had taken over her cabin. At first she was furious and took the buggy whip with her to drive them out of her cabin. Then as she almost kicked the front door open, she saw the small children sitting around on the dirt floor. The woman standing at the stove, looked as though she had been shot when Nadine burst into the one room cabin. Then she smiled and said, "I'll bet you are the lady who built this cabin and you are a wonderin what a bunch of squatters is a doin livin in youren house, aint choo?"

Nadine smelled the food cooking, and felt that the need was for her to relinquish the cabin to this family, "After all I came here to burn the cabin down, didn't I."

Nadine ask the lady, "Do you have pen, ink and paper?"

"Yess'um, sumers, here on the buffet." She handed the writing materials to Nadine and she sat down at the table and wrote.

"I, Nadine Workman do hereby deed without restriction the cabin and the amount of property that is belonging to Russell and Nadine Workman which the Land Office in Kissimmee will disclose to the bearer of this title and deed."

"What is your name?" How do you want the deed to read when you record it?" Nadine asked the lady who was starring at her with wide eyes.

"What do you want my . . . our'ens name fer maam?" the lady asked.

"Do you want this place? If you do give me your name so I can put it on the deed and I will give you the house and all the property that is owned by me and my dead husband," Nadine tried to snap the lady back into reality of some sort and when Nadine said, "dead husband," she gulped out a squeak then said, "My husband name ah James Bray and I be Olivia, thems my . . .

Ourn young'uns.

Nadine wrote the names on the deed, signed it and handed it to the lady, shook her hand and started out the door.

Olivia called, "Miss, I . . . jist . . . I guess I . . ." then she buried her face into the bottom of her apron and sobbed. The children all gathered around their mother and tried to console her as though they had seen this before and they did not understand that this crying was for pure joy and happiness.

Nadine muttered as she shut the door behind her, "Yeah I know."

Nadine was now in the seventh month of her pregnancy and was showing very much as she went from place to place but always back to the Tanners depot where she helped with the meals of the day.

It struck her strange that the baby was moving more now than ever before. And as she climbed into the carriage to go to the Stage depot she felt a small pain in the middle of her back. She just thought it was from the long buggy ride of the last two days and she had another two days in front of her now. She whipped up the horses and she decided to follow the railroad to Ft. Cummins, then take the Bent Penny Trace to the Bent Penny Ranch where she could get a meal and spend the night.

Darkness had fallen on the trail and the travelers as the evening with its purple, and pink skies turned into inky blackness. Nadine pulled the team up and got down to light the lantern so she could see the road that the horses were on.

The lantern light flickered into the scrub and was absorbed there as little of the light was returned. Strange shapes, and objects appeared, and disappeared as the horses dutifully drew the buggy along into the night.

Nadine had been dozing as the clip clop of the horses began to sing a rhythmic tune and it was as she was hypnotized by the patter of the horses hooves. Suddenly, she was jolted awake by a stabbing pain in her back that made her cry out. And as the pain was getting the best of her she saw the dim light of the night lanterns hanging on each side of the sign that read "Office" she knew that she was just minutes away from the Bent Penny Ranch.

She pulled the horses up at the hitching rail in front of the office and began to call out for someone to help her.

A PLACE IN THE SCRUB

Mary Sykes Remmick was the first to the buggy, as soon as Earl Ray got there she would have the young lady taken into the spare room for the night. Mary noticed that the lady was heavy with child, and thought that the time for the birth was near.

Orange Blossom seemed to appear out of nowhere, she was at the side of the young lady by the time Earl Ray had her on the bed. Mary and Blossom undressed the lady, and saw that there was blood coming from the birth canal.

Mary told Blossom, "Go to the kitchen and make hot tea and broth, as quickly as you can. Blossom took the order and made for the kitchen. Soon the hot tea was served on the wonderfully beautiful silver tea service; which was a wedding gift to Mary, when she was married to her first husband. Blossom just loved to serve tea in such an elegant tea service. Meanwhile the broth was being made by sealing raw beef in a Mason jar, boiling the jar in boiling water until the beef gave up its succulent juices, and allowed the young lady its life saving liquid.

"What's your name honey?" Mary asked

"Nadine Workman," she answered. Then she added, "I have been staying with the Tanners at the stage depot for several months and I decided the day before yesterday to go and settle my property worries then come back home to the Tanners stage depot and general store. Am I going to have my baby now? It really is too soon, you see, I think that I am only into my seventh month."

"I don't know child," Mary said then she placed her hand on her stomach to feel if the baby was moving, and promptly got a swift kick, which made Mary laugh out loud.

"Well if his kick is anything, then he will do what ever nature wants to do with the birth," Mary said in a matter of fact way. Then she picked up the sheet and covered the young lady's nude body. Then with two quilts she was bundled, to keep her and the baby warm.

"I hear a buggy coming up to the yard," Blossom said as she put the Indian blanket over all the other covers on Nadine. Blossom looked at Nadine and said, "You rest."

The dogs seldom come from under the porch to bark at anyone, but this time they did.

"Git back under at poach and not a-nother bark out'en you or I git my whip," Jeremiah yelled at the dogs as he stepped onto the porch from the office.

"Well if it aint doc Zimmerman whot choo doin this side o Kissimmee?" Jeremiah asked as he took the tie down from the bridle and wrapped it over the hitching rail, on the right hand side of the porch steps, which led to the office.

"You know you might jist be heer by provee-dence. You know whot doc, we got our'en selfs an preg-ant female woman and Mary and Blossom is a tendin ov her now," Jeremiah told the doctor as he shook his hand and helped him from the buggy at the same time.

"What other kind of a woman would be pregnant than a female? I was hoping for a cup of coffee and a piece of Mary's peacan pie, before I started my trip to Bartow," the doctor said as he climbed the three steps, and was herded through the office and into the hall that led to the dining hall, then into the guestroom. On each side of the hall are the rooms, on the left is the guestroom and on the right is the room now occupied by Earl Ray and Mary, the room at one time had been Mr. Allbritton's bed room. One door led directly into the office next to the old roll top desk.

"I see by the large bump in the covers that you are the patient," the doctor said to Nadine as he sent all the men out of the room, then pulled the covers from Nadine, and began his examination.

In about twenty minutes the doctor walked into the dining room and sat at the tables end nearest the kitchen door where his hot coffee and peacan pie awaited him.

"Well, you will have to wait for the baby another month or two as she isn't ready to have the, or those babies. I faintly heard two or more heart beats but I can't be sure if it wasn't an echo from the other side of the womb. I would like another exam in a few days to see if there is any movement to the extra heart beats," the Doctor explained to the sleepy faces in front of him, then said, "Go on to bed, she isn't going to have the baby tonight or anytime very soon."

"Doctor can she drive her buggy on to the Tanners Stagecoach Depot tomorrow, or should she stay here and let us send a message to them by Ole Mossy Back or Efrim when they drive up with the stagecoach?" Mary asked the doctor.

"She can drive in a day or two as soon as she has stopped bleeding for twenty-four hours," the Doctor explained to the group seated at the table, and by this time meant almost everyone at the compound.

"Mary, I am going to lie down on your sofa for a few minutes and then go on to Bartow," the Doctor said and went into the living room and literally flopped down on the sofa.

The rooster crowed and the doctor awoke with a start, jumped up and looked for his bag but when he smelled the coffee and breakfast he decided to linger a few minutes longer and would check in on Nadine once more, before he would eat and run.

Nadine was up and helping the ladies in the kitchen when the doctor came into the dining room, looked then shouted, "Young lady, you just go now, and get back into the bed for at least two more days. If you start to hemorrhage we will not be able to save the babies. Now go."

Silence had fallen over the dining room when the doctor admonished Nadine to go back to bed, but the big silencer was the word "BABIES_" as in more than one, the last multiple births was when the twins were born to Davy and Brittany Pearce, some six or seven years back.

The din from the men and ladies talking resumed, and now it was about the multiple babies to be born in the scrub again.

At sun up the doctor found his buggy hitched and ready, Old Will Henry and John Henry had stabled his horses the night before, fed and given them water and hay while they brushed them and put them in stalls for the balance of the night.

A slap on the rump and the horses were turning onto the trace headed for Bartow.

A quarter till two the doctor pulled up in front of the depot and hitched his horses to the rail out front then climbed the steps to the general store. He was met with a lot of smiles and joy in seeing him keep his rounds. He went straight to Spurgeon and Maude Elsie and said, "There is a young woman named Nadine, who is at the Bent Penny Ranch and she started having a problem the day before yesterday and made it to the ranch in time. I have her on strict bed rest until the bleeding completely stops for twenty-four hours. Then she will be able to drive her buggy back here and there should be no more problems until the babies are born in just a few days short of two months."

Maude Elsie and Savannah, were the only two that caught, "BABIES," then they said, "Doctor did you say babies?"

"Yes, yes I think I heard two or more heart beats, however it could be the echo of the heart against the wall of the womb, at this time I am uncertain as to the number of babies," the doctor said as he picked up the coffee that Savannah had poured for him. He took the cup and saucer and sat at the long table.

"I have given her permission to drive her buggy back home as soon as she has stopped bleeding for twenty-four hours, but if there is someone who could drive her it would be a lot easier on her and they must drive slowly. It might take two days to get here from Bent Penny Ranch," the doctor concluded, then took a sip of the hot coffee and accepted the plate of meat and vegetables offered by Savannah, then she topped his coffee cup off and placed the coffee pot near the doctor and sat down to listen to the story of what Nadine had been through the last week, when she had gone to Davenport to clear up the property problem.

"Who ya rec'on ah kin go fetch at aire Nadine an her buggy," Spurgeon asked as he sat at the table too and reached for the coffee pot. But Savannah already had it in her hand, she poured a cup for him and he promptly poured the hot coffee into his saucer and blew on the hot liquid, then slurped the coffee this way until the cup was empty.

"I will go for her and bring her back as soon as the stagecoach headed for Ft. Cummings gets here."

It was Claude Hayman, who had just returned from New Orleans, through Tampa and the stage had brought him here that morning.

"She won't be able to be moved for at least two more days," Maude Elsie told the young man. Then she asked, "do you mind sleeping in the bunk house, we won't charge you for that, just for the meals you eat while you are here."

"That's alright with me and I will take the next stage from Tampa. May I get a few things from the store?" Claude agreed.

"Shore ya kin sonny jist com'on wiff me," Spurgeon said as he stepped over to the store.

The young man bought a colt pistol and a winchester rifle both in forty-five caliber long colt, and he bought a saddle bridle and all the trappings of a man who had decided to drift for a while rather than settle in the near by settlement.

Then he asked Spurgeon, "Why don't you have a telegraph line put into here? The company would put you in a Western Union office and you could keep in touch with all your coaches along the route."

"I haint never thot bout no telly-graph place here in the scrub. 'Bout how much ya thank hit'll cos' me ta git a telly-graph war hitched in heer at tha depot?" Spurgeon asked.

"Well I heard that the Bent Penny was going to have one installed so they could check on the cattle markets before they herded their cows to the shipping pens on the coast. So it would just about cost nothing to bring a Western Union office into your depot. As a mater of fact Western Union might even install the service for free. Of course you will have to have a telegrapher to operate the Western Union office for you, and that's where I come in. I am a telegrapher and since I haven't heard from the railroad I might as well go to work for Western Union." Claude made a good case for himself and before long he had sold Spurgeon on the idea and now he would go to work on Maude Elsie.

"I seen tha way you has looked at Savannah, aire ya shore hit aint her'en yoo done a hankerin fer?" Spurgeon asked Claude.

Claude blushed and shuffled his feet, but couldn't answer Spurgeon.

"Uh, huh, ats whot ah done thot, at yoose was a lookin on Savannah a awful lot with rooster eyes," Spurgeon teased the young man who took it in stride and laughed when Spurgeon finally let up on the lad.

Spurgeon told Maude Elsie about the Western Union idea and soon they had Claude writing letters to the company trying to get the application in at the same time the Ranch did theirs.

The morning came the day before Nadine was to come home, but Claude would ride the stagecoach to the Bent Penny Ranch, and wait for Nadine to be cleared by Mary Remmick.

In the mean time he sold the telegraph system to Mary, Earl Ray and Jeremiah, Davy Pearce, put his two cents worth in and said he wanted the wire at the salt plant too. But he could act as his own telegrapher and the ranch's too when they got the system installed.

A day and a night passed quickly and soon Claude was readying the buggy for their trip to the Tanners depot and general store.

The folks from the Bent Penny Ranch stood on the porch and waved good-by to Nadine and Claude.

As they traveled the sun was relentless on the pair and when they reached the next hammock Claude stopped the buggy and drew the top over the seats and rolled up the isinglass side curtains, so if it rained they could be dry and snug behind the curtains.

Getting back into the buggy and slapping the reins on the horses rumps they started out pulling easy and smooth.

Out of the scrub came three cowboys and with their whips they caused Nadine's team to shy back and forth shaking her up pretty bad. When she moaned, Claude handed her the reins and told her to hold them steady for just a moment.

Claude picked up his rifle and jacked a round into the chamber. And said, "Now boys I don't have a whip but this winchester will make about as much noise. Anyone want to challenge this? If not you all go back into your scrub and try to scare someone else, but you better mind out, they might shoot instead of talk. Now what is you boy's decision?"

"Let's go, they aint no fun, no how," the oldest boy said as they wheeled their horses around and went back into the scrub. But Claude waited until he could not hear them riding and talking through the scrub. He sat down un-cocked the rifle an laid it back between the seats and stuck the colt back into the holster next to the rifle. He took the reins from Nadine's hands and clucked the horses onto the road.

Nadine had not said a word all through the confrontation with the scrub cowboys. She soon broke the silence and said, "Weren't you afraid of those men? They could have hurt you with those whips, are you some type of gunman?" Nadine looked into his eyes and saw a tender man, who was just protecting their own rights.

"No maam, I'm no kind of gunman, as a mater of fact I just bought the guns from Spurgeon the day before yesterday and I have had about two hours, and three boxes of cartridges of practice. So most of my action was bluff. I noticed that they only had rifles and they were in the scabbard attached to the saddle. Also they were far enough away that they couldn't reach me with a twenty foot whip. So I basically had what Mr. Colt called "Gun Brevity" and that is what I knew; if I had the loudest voice I would win that argument."

THE TWO JOBS

At a half passed noon, the second day, the buggy with Nadine and Claude trotted into the side yard of the depot and general store. Claude reined up just next to the side steps going up into the store. Then he jumped down and went to help Nadine to the first step then with her on his arm, marched up the steps to the screen door and opened it, and took Nadine through it, turned and went back to the buggy, to get Nadine's bags, as he stood in the store with the bags, and wanted to take them to Nadine's room. Spurgeon took the bags to Maude Elsie as Claude waited to see if she was alright. When Spurgeon came back into the store he told Claude that she had gone to bed and she would see him again at suppertime. Claude walked out and down the stairs to the buggy, he took the lead and walked the buggy to the barn. He left the top up and rolled and fastened the curtains down, put the horses into the stalls and started to brush them. One of the cow hands came in and pitched the horses some hay and fed them a ration of oats and corn.

Claude was wearing his colt on his hip and the rifle was leaning inside the barn door, the door opened the three men who stopped them in the scrub walked into the barn. One of the men saw the rifle and picked it up pointing it at the cow hand, ordered him out of the barn. He left by a side door, and Claude glanced, and saw him headed for the store.

The three men expressed their displeasure at being taken down in front of the lady like they had been.

Claude knew that there was no bullet in the chamber of the rifle, so he started to the stall gate and saw that the fellow doing all the talking was there at the gate, Claude poked the horse with a spur he had taken from his boot, the horse kicked the gate and flung it open catching the man by the shirt sleeve, spinning him around and as the other two watched their partner getting the swing of his life, Claude stepped out into the barn and pulled the colt at the same time.

"You kids are the poorest bandits, that ever has been in the scrub. You are dumb too, as you are figured out, every time you act or react. I knew what you were and weren't going to do. I knew that you could not swing a whip as there was no room for a whip longer than six foot. And you didn't have a gun until you took mine up, then you didn't jack a round into the chamber, so you all are, are losers all the way around".

"Whot's a goin on heer," Spurgeon asked Claude as he walked up behind the three men with his double barrell shot gun.

"We have a trio of men, who came out of the scrub yesterday, and I got the best of them, now we have the second go round with them today." Claude explained.

"Is they tha ones?" surprised, Spurgeon asked. Nadine was a tellin us 'bout that when Amos come in tellin me three men had you hold up in tha barn. But you got them hold up aint choo?"

"What do we do with these desperados, Mr. Tanner?"

"Let's put 'em in tha smoke house and I'll git Amos to go fine them hosses what them fellers rode in on. After them fellers toll us'ens whar they leff um at in tha scrub," Spurgeon decided.

The smoke house was built out of hewn oak boards and were nearly six inches thick, the door was large and the whole building was nearly air tight, but for the chimney on the opposite side of the room from the door. There were hooks with hams, bacon sides, ribs, and sausage. The men were told that they knew exactly what was hanging and stored in the smoke house and if any was missing when the sheriff took them away they, would lose their horses for what ever was missing. They would be fed and given plenty of water but only fed once a day until the lawman came.

A bucket of water was set inside the smoke house and soon Amos came up with their horses. Spurgeon told him to feed and brush them, then let them loose in the ready lot. The horses were not broken to wagon but they seemed to be good saddle horses.

"I'll take one of their horses and go to Bartow and get the Sheriff in the morning and I will also check on the applications for the Western Union wire," Claude told Spurgeon. Then he went inside to check on Nadine.

A few minutes later he met Savannah in the store and asked, "Would you go for a walk with me after supper?" Savannah agreed and went back toward the kitchen. She looked back just before she entered the door beyond the diningroom.

Claude rode up in front of the sheriff's office and hitched the horse to the rail, a man came out of the office and onto the sidewalk then he looked at the horse that Claud had ridden in on and went back into the sheriff's office. Then reappeared with the sheriff in tow.

"Where'd you get this horse, son," the sheriff asked.

"I got it from one of three that were ridden into the Tanners depot and store yesterday. They tried to hold me up in the scrub, between Bent Penny Ranch on the Trace, a ways before the depot and store. Then they tried to do something yesterday and that got them locked up into the Tanners smoke house.," Claude explained, then added, "That is why I have this horse tied up in front of your office, sheriff."

"The horse is from the Stuart place and this is the foreman of the place," the sheriff told Claude.

"What happened?" Claude asked the foreman.

"I hired three young men to drive cows from the scrub to the ranch and when I furnished them the horses and saddles they went out and we never saw hide nor hair of the horses nor the men." the foreman told Claude.

"Well I can tell you, where all their hide and hair is," Claude told the foreman, he and the sheriff laughed at the idea of them being held in the smoke house.

"Maude Elsie will be glad for you to take them off her hands, she's just feeding them enough to keep them alive, anyhow," Claude told the sheriff.

"I'm kinda short on help right now so I will deputize you and give you enough manacles to keep them from any monkey business while you escort them back here for trial. What's your name? The sheriff asked Claude.

"Claude Hayman, sir," he answered.

"Can you write readin? The sheriff asked.

"Yes . . . yes sir sheriff," Claude answered, not knowing where the sheriff was going with his questions.

"Aw right then, you write down ever thing you told me and so the Judge will know that it was wrote by your hand only," the sheriff answered then turned to the Stuart Foreman and asked him the same questions. But the foreman couldn't write anything but his own name; the sheriff asked Claud if he would write what the foreman had to say about the men stealing their three horses.

Claude agreed and since the horse he rode in on was dead heading back to the Stuart Ranch, he would have plenty of time to write what the man told him while he waited for the stage to arrive from Tampa in the late afternoon. Claude wrote the words and put as much emphasis on the facts of the men not preforming their duties they were hired for. Then he started to write his story and what had happened in the scrub and later at the barn at the Tanner's depot settlement.

Claude was the talk of the town while he was in Bartow, even the ladies of the Baptist church wanted to know what that handsome young man was doing wandering around on the side walks of the town, when all Claude was doing was walking from the sheriff's office, to the café two blocks away.

The town was clean, the buildings were mostly of brick and mortar with cement sidewalks, since it was the county seat, most of the people in the town were Lawyers, Judges, clerks, or elected officials, or people who worked for lawyers, Judges, clerks or elected officials. The shop keepers, bartenders, hotel people, and all the others, didn't have the time to be milling about the town.

Claude walked by the Western Union office, and that reminded him of the promise he made to Spurgeon. He walked in and asked for the manager. There were only two persons in the office, both wore long sleeves with garters keeping them from slipping and getting into the telegraph keys as the men tapped out messages, the other wrote messages that were incoming. Both wore green eye shades, so nothing was there to give away who was the ramrod of this outfit.

It turned out to be the man who was recording the incoming messages, who stood up, looked Claude up and down. Then asked, "Looking for a job, young man?"

"No sir, I wrote letters of application for the Bent Penny Ranch, the Tanners Stage Depot, and the salt works out on the Trace and since I have come to Bartow on business I thought it would be prudent to inquire about the disposition of the two applications." Claude answered.

"Oh, yes, now let me see what did I do with those letters? I keep them on file and as we get the answers we jot them down on the letters in the files," the manager said as he went to the wooden file drawer, then bringing three files at the same time, laid them on the marble counter.

There they were the certificates from Western Union, they had been sent by the mail and from the looks of the files they had been here for a while.

"When did you get these certificates?" Claude asked.

"Well sir, . . . let's see now, . . . according to the time and date stamp we got them the day before yesterday, they came by stagecoach mail," the man said as he stamped them with his rubber stamp, then handed them to Claude.

"Lend me your telegraphers catalog, I will order what is needed to set up the Western Union at the depot and the ranch offices," Claude asked the man.

Claude made the order, it was being tapped out on the key in the Western Union office as he walked out of the office and onto the sidewalk. He pulled his watch out of its pocket and noted that he had fifteen minutes to walk the two blocks to the stagecoach depot. But first he had to go by the sheriff's office and get his badge and shackles and hand cuffs. He threw the lawman's hardware in a burlap bag that was beside the sheriffs desk, pinned on the badge, swore the oath of office and literally ran the block down to the stage depot where the stage was waiting.

Claude thought, "I am really going to get the ribbing from Mossy Back and Efrim about the badge, but I'll leave it on anyway and get it over with on the way to the depot at Tanners store."

He was right, Mossy Back and Efrim tossed little quips back and forth about the gun toten lawman and telegraph operator him using the smoke house for a jail and on and on it went until almost midnight the stage pulled up in front of the depot.

"All out fer tha night, tha men'll gote the bunkhouse and kin use inny bed whot aint got no body in it or iffen hits warm neether, cuz the feller whot made hit warm might be at the privy and he wont take good to you abe'en in hissens bed." Mossy Back yelled out just as though it was high noon or something. If he woke up a few people it was of no concern of his for he had a job to do and yelling at the horses, mules or people was part of his job.

Swimming from the ride and the rocking of the stage Claude stumbled as he stepped out of the coach and went sprawling in the white sand of the depot dooryard. Then the chiding started again from Mossy and Efrim. "A man with two jobs should oughta stan'o hissens own two legs, but the new badge was whot dun pult him over cuz hit makes 'im top heavy, don't choo know." And the teasing went on.

"What's this about a badge?" Maude Elsie asked Claude as she poured him a cup of coffee and pushed a plate of food in front of him.

"Yes maam, the sheriff wanted me to be legal when I bring these three men to Bartow on the stage tomorrow," Claude said, then he told her about the other two horses and saddles that had to be returned to the Stuart Ranch. "I'll continue there after I drop the prisoners off at the sheriff's office." Claude concluded.

"Why aint choo hitch up the buggy and drive it a hind tha stage with tha horses and saddles tied ta tha buggy. An let them prisoner fellers ride in the stagecoach, why don cha?" Spurgeon spoke as he walked into the kitchen and poured himself a cup of coffee. "Its a gonna be three more days cause I lost a driver team to the railroad lass week and Mossy and Efrim been workin seven day til ah kin fine some nuther drivers," he sat down at the table and drank his coffee.

THE PROGRESS IN THE SCRUB

The scrub was quiet as the dawn was opening a new day, the scrub jays flew form tree to tree looking for food or acorns and calling to its mate, as other animals began looking for a quiet place to rest from their night of stalking about foraging for food.

The horse snorted as it was led to the stagecoach for the days trips. The trace chains clinked with the tune of the scrub jay and echoed up to the scrub. A new morning was beginning at Tanner's depot and general store.

The horses were hitched and the stagecoach was ready to go to Bartow. The drivers climbed to their box seat and waited.

Spurgeon walked out to the smokehouse and unlocked the padlock on the heavy door. The prisoners rubbed their eyes and walked out of their confinement. Each stood up strait for the first time in five days, stretched and swung their arms as if to get the circulation going again. The handcuffs and manacles had been left in-place and now made it difficult to walk and it would be impossible to mount into the stagecoach. As each was led to the privy the other two had to stand with their feet one pace back from a pine tree with his head against the pine tree. The men who were guarding them were taking no chances of their running. After the privy time they were walked single file to the wash stand and were told to, "Wash up_"

They were served breakfast of hotcakes with cane syrup and black coffee. After they had washed their dishes and utensils they were in single file again headed for the stagecoach. Seeing that they would have to remove the leg irons, Spurgeon hastily stacked several wooden crates up to the stagecoach's steps, this allowed the three prisoners to take small steps and still walk up to and enter the stagecoach door without removing the leg irons. The two horses were tied to the stake on the rear of the stage and Claude mounted his horse and waved the drivers on to move out for the trip to the sheriff's office in Bartow.

The stage pulled into Bartow at two a. m. sharp, Claude walked over to the sheriff's office and knocked on the door. Stanley Melrose himself opened the door and helped the prisoners down from the coach. They were indeed most happy to see the jail cell for there was a bed in each cell and they immediately took to them with their clothes on, and were asleep and snoring before they had their leg iron and handcuffs off.

"They smell like bar-b-que," Mel said as he locked the last cell door.

"Spurgeon had them locked in his smokehouse," Claude answered.

"You gonna stay for the trial, or are you going right back to the settlement?" Mel asked.

"I'm going to get a hotel room and finish the night out there then I've other business here in Bartow, then I need to travel to Lakeland for some business. Do you want the deputy badge back now, Mel?" Claude stated.

"Naw, as a matter of fact I would like for you to keep the badge until you have to go to work for the Western Union," Mel told Claude.

Mossy and Efrim thanked Mel for the coffee and Mel thanked them for their help in unloading the prisoners and told them to, "come back anytime."

"Not so lackly," Mossy muttered as he went out the door.

"Me too," Efrim said to back up what Mossy said.

Mel and Claude had to laugh as they could see how uneasy the two drivers were in the sheriff's office and jail.

Mel told his deputy, "Take the two Stuart horses to the livery stable and have Buddy put them up and charge the fee to the Stuart ranch."

As Claude walked down the street to the hotel the deputy walked past him headed for the livery another block away. Claude noticed that there was an echo in the early morning between the buildings in Bartow, he also noted the fog rolling in.

Claude signed the register and climbed the stairs to his assigned room, looked out the windows and saw that it was a sixteen foot drop to the ground and no one would try to come in the window to his room. He locked the door and fell exhausted on to the bed in his clothes too. He woke up an hour later and removed his boots then slept soundly until the sun was shining in his windows.

Claude went down to breakfast in the hotel café and noticed a man with a smudged buckskin jacket on and he recognized him as Billy Matson from the Bent Penny Ranch, because he had hauled freight for the ranch. Billy would be a good prospect to haul the poles and equipment to the two stations for Western Union. He walked up to the young man and introduced himself to Billy and asked if he might sit down and talk to him about a hauling job.

Billy looked interested and gestured for Claude to sit with him. Billy noticed the deputy's badge and Claude pulled it off and dropped it into his shirt pocket.

"Billy, if you know it or not the telegraph is coming to the Bent Penny ranch and also to the stage depot at the Tanner's depot and general store on the Bent Penny Trace. I have ordered telegraph poles, wire, insulators, and a lot of other gear that will be necessary to run the wires to the two stations. The wires will take off from Bartow and will be installed into the stage depot first then about one to two months longer will be at the ranch. We will need you and several other wagons to bring in the poles from Ft. Cummins rail side. Some of the poles can be cut from cypress and slash pine but they won't last very long in the ground so we will have to replace them pretty soon with the ones from Sanford, treated with creosote and coal tar to make them last longer in the Florida climate. Are you interested in hauling for this special event?" Claude had laid it all out for Billy and he sipped his coffee and waited for Billy's answer.

"Well, sir you know I have a steady haul for Mr. Davy Crocket at the Bent Penny and he uses my wagons to haul his salt to Tampa and I brang hay an' feed fer the cows and horses back. So ah haint got no empty runs, so's ah cud git poles an' sumthin else lack war an stuff lack that.

Ah'll haft ax Mr. Davy bout hit though." Billy replied.

"Sure Billy you check with Davy and in the mean time I will see if I can meet up with a few other teamsters in the Tampa area who could help supply the wire line. We will need three to four hundred wagon loads of poles alone." Claude needed to get some type of answer before he went to other markets for the wagons.

"Oh, by-the-way, Billy, asked Davy if he can stop by the depot to see me the first chance he gets." Claude thought of the survey crew and there would be plenty of surveying and engineering to get the telegraph wires in to the new stations.

Several days passed and the wagon drivers and teamsters began showing up at the depot, some driving out of their way to see what was going on with the Western Union guy at the stage depot. Claude had printed flyers that explained the entire need of the wagons, but for the teamsters who could not read, he read aloud the circular and asked that they give him their names and addresses so he could reach them later when the engineering and surveying had been accomplished.

The plan was for three carloads of poles to come to the railroad depot at Ft. Cummings first, followed by all the wire, insulators, batteries, switches and battery acid on the next car. Then the balance of the poles until the project was finished.

Davy Crocket Pearce met with Claude several times and agreed to allow Billy Matson to move some of the poles and then assist the wire teams in getting to the sites.

Claude had mastered the liaison between the teamsters and the railroad and Davy's surveying and engineering. The entire program was planned like a military plan for an up coming battle; with all elements ready for the first carload of poles to arrive at Ft. Cummins depot.

Old Will Henry, Willie Mae Luke and John Henry Luke had hired out to work the chuck wagons to feed the hungry linemen and surveyors. Mary Sykes Remmick and Maude Elsie Tanner kept the supplies rolling to the depot's strung out along the lines and still maintained their work at the ranch and depot.

1891 was the year that the first pole was put into the ground and the telegraph line began to web its way from Bartow toward the depot along the Bent Penny Trace. More and more change order notices came from Western Union to branch to Florence Villa and along the railroad right-of-way.

Mr. Henry Plant had finished his railroad from Ft. Cummings to Plant City and on to Tampa. There was a small line which came along the land bridge from Mulberry's Bone Valley, the W&BV ran now bringing phosphate from Bone Valley to the phosphate docks at Tampa's Seddon Island. This short line railroad ran to Bartow and connected with the

Atlantic Coast Line and the Seaboard railroads. Now the passengers could travel from Jacksonville to Bartow and Ft. Meade by train cheaper than the stagecoach fare.

Spurgeon and Maude Elsie saw the writing on the wall and began to look into other possibilities. Spurgeon still hunted cows in the scrub and knew that would be a source of income until the stage line could be taken out of service or shortened to just Ft. Cummins to Bent Penny Ranch then to the depot at the settlement and on to Bartow. It was not necessary to run all the way to Tampa since the trains ran on a schedule now.

There was an un-noticed influx of settlers in the scrub now and when realization came to Maude Elsie and Spurgeon the general store was doing better and they were running out of items almost every week causing them to double and re-double their orders to the warehouses in Tampa and Kissimmee. Meat seemed to be the one item that they were out of mostly. So Spurgeon rigged up a place down near the bayhead that could be used as his slaughter house and he could butcher several cows a day and a hog every day that kept the smoke house busy and their three boys could hunt for game around the scrub. They brought in deer, turkey, wild hogs, rabbits, ducks, and wild chickens.

Maude Elsie decided to fence in a place to keep chickens and inside her one hundred feet by one hundred feet compound they put in fifty head of wild chickens and one wild rooster. The rooster was meaner than a Mexican bull, and every bit as willing to fight anyone or any thing that went inside that chicken pen. After a fortnight wooden crates were placed in the chicken pen for the hens to lay their eggs. All of the meat, eggs, wild meats, smoked meat, hams, bacon and sausages were helping the general store to come to life and make a profit for Maude Elsie and Spurgeon.

The stagecoach business was relegated to a small area in the front northeastern corner of the depot and the balance of the depot was becoming a rooming house and café. Home cooked meals and a never ending supply of smoked meats from the smoke house and the garden too.

There was a lot of good that came from the chicken pen as the manure was used to fertilize the garden and the muck from the stalls kept the corn and peas and beans happy and growing.

But for that rooster, no one ever made friends with him, until Maude Elsie made chicken and dumpling out of him and his kind in that yard.

LEAVE IT TO THE WOMEN

Maude Elsie, Savannah and Nadine, all had a hand in the transforming the depot into a boarding house, and Outsiders came here to eat when they had to travel two more hours to get to the depot, for those scrumptious meals the ladies cooked up three times a day except on Sunday.

By this time the ladies were running three chuck wagons a week to the linemen and the "holers" as they were called which was short for "gopher holers" were the men who dug holes for the telegraph poles to go into the ground. They would dig a hole straight down four feet then on one side of the hole (normally where the pole was) they would dig a slanting hole to the bottom of the post hole. This gave an angle of about thirty degrees when the pole was placed into the gopher hole. Then the pole was righted, with pike poles. The pike poles were long wooden shafts with sharp metal spike on the end which would dig into the wooden pole and two men could stand the telegraph pole upright while the tamper would fill in the hole with dirt until the pole was set. Climbers could climb the pole as soon as the tamper walked away toward the next pole.

The chuck wagon now had a trailer wagon which carried the folding tables and chairs for the men to sit at and eat their meals on white ironed table clothes for every meal. That touch stopped any of the men living near by from bringing their lunch. When the meal was finished the men folded the tables and chairs and stored them in the trailer wagon for the ladies to move on to the next stop which would be coffee at four o:clock p.m.

As was the normal week, Mondays were wash days and Tuesday ironing, Wednesday baking day, Thursday clean the house, Friday strip and make the beds with fresh linens. The chuck wagons and the boarding house were bringing in more and more profits, and one day Maude Elsie sat down to rest for a few minutes, looked at Savannah and Nadine and said, "Why are we killing ourselves doing all of this cooking, washing, ironing, baking and cleaning when we are making enough that we could hire a couple of women to help us in this work. Now the next time you go out on the chuck wagon you stop and ask every squatter if they want to work for wages and if so come talk to me. If they are dirty or have too many children then just pass them by and go on to the next. I know that there are some people who would like to work for wages."

The next Monday there were about twenty women and five men who turned up to get some work of any kind. Maude Elsie and Nadine sat at the tables and took names and where the people lived. They hired seven people this time, four women and three men. The three men, Chandler "Jake" Owen, Brokowski "Ski" Shalen, Norman "Norm" Tracy, started immediately as the wood pile was seriously low. Two men began hauling trees in from the scrub the other sawed the trees to stove wood size and then started to split the logs until the men drug up another log. There was some oak but mostly pine as it burned hotter and would light the oak or hickory hard woods.

Since this was Monday the four women; Eunice "Eunie" Dunbar, Gladys Selmon, Birtayful "Birdie" Ort, Hazelma "Dixie" Dicksey, started to get ready to wash the linen table clothes and they had to be a sparking white. They would boil the table clothes first, then other item such as the bed sheets and pillow cases, then the clothes were boiled; this way the water did not have to be changed in the wash pot, just more cold water added when it was needed. The next day Tuesday, the women ironed all day long and finally about dark Maude Elsie came in from the day's run on the chuck wagon to find a nice supply of clean table clothes and leave the soiled ones which could not be folded and used again for the women to wash, dry, and iron the next day.

On Wednesday the house smelled of yeast as bread dough was rising in the pans and were ready for the oven. The four women worked as a team and got the chores done in the house while the bread was rising and the fresh table clothes ironed, folded and placed in the hall for the next days chuck wagon.

The wood pile kept dwindling to the dangerously low when Spurgeon went to the line boss and asked him if he would help and send what ever men he could to assist getting the wood pile back to the place where the three men could handle it. The line boss told him they would be happy to if they would have more pecan pies on the dessert menu.

The next morning there were two pole wagons full of wood ready to be split and stacked in to the one chord ricks. The three men quickly split the wood and soon were two chords ahead of the game. The next day there were three wagons of cut wood, and so on, until there were ten chords of split wood on hand. But with the washing every day and what was burned in the cook stove the strain on the three men was awesome and night fell many a time with the three still splitting wood.

The price of the meals was raised from fifteen cents to twenty cents and that included the pecan pies that were on the wagons every day. No one seemed to notice that the women were at the stove as early as four-thirty in the morning and did not leave until the supper dishes were washed, dried and put away in the cupboard. Any left overs went with the women and men who did the work to make the meal. The dogs got the bones and scraps that were left. And the hogs got the slop from the slop barrel that the women brought back on the chuck wagon. Nothing was wasted on that farm as everything was valuable to someone or something.

The line bosses began to furnish the many blocks of ice needed for the water barells and as the ice wagon brought six hundred pounds of ice each day the women would put one fifty pound block in the tea after they sweetened it with the sugar. For a fifty gallon barrel of tea would take twenty pounds of sugar. With the sloshing of the tea in the barrel it was plenty cold when it reached its destination and the hot, tired, thirsty men drank nearly all of the iced tea at dinner time.

By the end of the year the wire was nearly done and the telegraph was click clacking away at the Bent Penny ranch and at the depot boarding house. There were fewer linemen now as they were thinning out since the poles had all been set and what was left was finishing the wire and replacing a few insulators which trigger happy cowboys were using for target practice. One line wagon would work the trace every week and keep the lines singing in the summer air. It seemed to draw birds also as the two wires stretched from pole to pole would see it black with crows and in the summer a few mocking birds and such would sit on the wire watching for a hapless bug that might wander into their field of vision.

As the production of the telegraph wires and poles began to wane the women at the ranch and the depot began cutting back on the amount of stores they put in to supply the chuck wagons but the meals, quality and quantity did not drop off as did the men who were originally eating them. There was no way that one chuck wagon could feed the men on both sides of the trace from the Bent Penny ranch, so the two kept sending out chuck wagon until the line boss told them to stop. There would be too few men to justify sending a wagon out to feed them.

Reluctantly the chuck wagons were refitted to go on the cattle drives and it came to Mary Sykes Remmick that they could not justify the cost of a chuck wagon on the drives so she engaged Maude Elsie and the ladies to furnish chuck for the hungry cowboys on the drive from Bent Penny ranch to the port of Tampa, or Punta Rassa. The cattle were herded to the depot and set out to pasture on the flats just northwest of the depot. With drovers riding night guard the others could eat a good meal at the boarding house and sleep there if they wished but had to be ready to go at three-thirty the next morning. Breakfast, then to the herd, where the night guard was relieved to spend the day sleeping at the boarding house then catch up to the herd by late afternoon that day.

The next chuck would be ten to twelve miles ahead of the drive and the chuck wagon would be set up and the meal ready for the cowboys. If the drive was slower than that the chuck wagon would go back to the herd and they would eat later than noon, perhaps two to three in the afternoon. Then forward to the next chuck stop or supper, where the cows would be bedded down for the night. This gave the cowboys time to care for their horses and leather tack.

A roster was used to keep track of who worked when and what day they must ride night guard, so the men stayed busy and worked hard in the Florida climate, flora and fauna. The men who were working at the depot were now hired on as drovers for the drove this Spring now were finding out that there was life other than the hard work of sawing and splitting wood. It seemed that one or the other was finding without looking, all types of animals that would seek and harm the cattle in the herd as it drifted toward the west coast of Florida.

Jake Owen was keeping the bunch critters moving from outside the herd, about fifty yards, when he heard something running through the scrub. Not being able to see what it was he spurred his drove mule up and left the bunch critters to get to the main herd quickly. He cut the trail about the same time the wild bull did, now he dared not move as the bull had not seen the cows yet, only heard and smelled them. With nostrils flared and his mouth drooling, Jake felt that the bull might be rabid, he whistled his dog and told him to, "Sic em," and the dog sprang out after the scrub wild bull. As the dog grabbed the bull by the nose the bull flung its head and threw the dog into the palmetto patch some twenty feet north of the trail. With a whimper the dog came out of the scrub and lowered his head to guage what the bull would do next. It just stood there with its flared nostrils and ears laying back along its neck. Jake whistled the dog back, but this was not something the dog was apt to heed this time, for the dog had now developed a grudge against that bull and he was determined to put the bull on the ground to be marked, castrated, and a worm pill shoved up its butt. This dog was about to fight a bull twenty, thirty, times his weight.

The dog took up a crouching position, about twenty feet in front of the bull, and little by little he would creep up a few inches and each time he did the bull would paw the ground and back away a foot of two. At one time the bull looked away and when he did the dog was on him and had him by the throat. The bull reared and the dog held on. This time Jake could see the panic in the bulls eyes as he realized that he couldn't breathe and what breath he had he let out in a beller like scream.

That noise brought Earl Ray and Jeremiah up to where Jake was and as they came with their Marsh Tackies in a dead run, they saw the bull and the dog fight.

As the bull succumbed to the grip on his throat and the lack of air went to his knees then with a jerk fell to the ground. Jake whistled the dog off again but the bull did not breathe. Earl Ray ran up to the bull and kicked him in the stomach causing the bull to inhale air and start breathing again. The three men quickly built a brush arbor corral and herded the bull into it with the dog to guard him. The bull no longer the valiant began grazing from the grass and bushes in the corral.

Jake spurred up his mule and went back to recovering his bunch critters.

BLOOD IN THE SCRUB

Maude Elsie had gone into the store house when she saw a man running through the scrub and another chasing him. She screamed at Spurgeon to come quick. As Spurgeon ran out the backdoor of the depot the man circled around and fell at Maude Elsie's feet. His throat was cut but not deep enough to cut any vital veins or arteries. Just the same he was bleeding profusely and the bleeding had to be stopped. Spurgeon held his hand over the mans neck and tried to stop the bleeding by direct pressure. Maude Elsie in the mean time had grabbed a fishing pole from the rack beside the store house and began gathering spider webs from along the eaves of the store house. When she had what looked like a hat full of the webs she spread them on the man's neck and the bleeding subsided then stopped. Ski Shalen and Norm Tracy came up to the site and Maude Elsie told them of the second man who was chasing this man when she called for help.

The three men scanned the scrub for the sight of another man but saw no one. They walked out into the scrub a few feet then from behind a large clump of palmettoes came an Indian with his knife still in his hand. The three men backed up to the scene of the other man on the ground. The Indian approached them and said that this was a very bad man and the Seminole wanted this man for the molestation of an Indian girl.

At that pointless effort went into the saving of the mans life than a few minutes ago.

"She's my daughter_" the man shouted as he held the spider webs in place on his slashed neck. Then he began to sob, "She's my daughter and my squaw has told her people that I was not her lover but the father of her child." The man tried to stand, the Indian lunged at him with the knife. But the crowd of men stopped him from finishing his seemingly misguided deed.

"Nokomo, is her name and the child is mine, she is afraid that if she admits that the child is from a white man the tribe will turn her out," the man said as he choked back more sobs.

Spurgeon spoke up and said, "One a yall boy's gote tha Bent Penny ranch and on the way try to find out whar that thar Chief Billy Bow Legs is camped at. We'uns shore done need to heer whut hisself is got ta say bout this here deal here."

The men assisted the man into the boarding house and they disarmed the Indian man, but the Indian would not leave, he just sat out on the ground and seemed to be waiting. Perhaps he decided that calling in Chief Billy Bow Legs was the best thing to do.

The man was dressed in buckskins and had a Seminole made cotton shirt on under the buckskin pull over.

By this time Maude Elsie and Savannah put a bandage around the man's neck and Savannah asked, "What is your name so we know who we are talking to. The young man looked at them as though he had seen a ghost.

"Are you Rickman, from Tennessee?" the man asked Jake Owen. Then he lapsed into unconsciousness and fell on the floor of the Depot boarding house.

"Who is Rickman?" Maude Elsie asked the people and no one answered so she let it rest.

"Now let's get him off of the floor and into one of the beds," Savannah Ford ordered the men, she was now in charge since she was a nurse; she began to remove the spider webs and noted that the wound had turned black from the dried blood and the spider webs that had adhered to his skin. After having seen the nature of the wound she wrapped it once more with white linen strips someone had handed her for this purpose.

Spurgeon found the mans "possibles bag" which should carry lead shot, percussion caps, a nipple tool, and a patch knife. None of these things were in the bag. The man was carrying the bag like a "hobo's bundle" it had a wallet with his name and address in the mountains of Tennessee.

Harold Richards of James Town, Tennessee. Other items were

twenty-four long colt bullets in caliber .45, a stub of a pencil, a folding Barlow knife, a bunch of keys held together with a raw hide thong. There were pieces of rag as though he used them for bullet patches. But there was no muzzle loading gun, powder, or shot in the "possibles bag" that a man by the name of Harold Richards carried slung over his shoulder like a bundle.

Two days later the dooryard of the depot came alive as the Indian who had tried to cut Harold's throat had gone and come back long before day break and built a fire apparently to roast a rabbit he had killed and skinned while he was in the scrub.

Spurgeon and Maude Elsie looked out the door and saw that it was the Chief Billy Bow Legs and most of his hunting party.

"Come in Chief, welcome to are home and business, we been happy to see you'ens and wont youren advice," Spurgeon said as he led the old Indian into the kitchen of the boardinghouse.

"Got coffee and sweet?" the chief asked.

The chief was now in his late eighties and was not as spry as he once was and Spurgeon remembered. Chief Billy Bow Legs was thin and his face very drawn but his dark eyes could pierce your soul with his stare or dance like a fairy, and on the rare times he laughed his eyes would show the merriment he enjoyed but seldom showed.

Nadine handed the chief a cup of coffee with the cup on a saucer. The Indian handed Nadine the saucer and took the sugar bowl from her hand. With the agility of a pickpocket he spooned seven or eight spoons of sugar into the coffee and drank it down, handed Nadine the cup and asked for more.

"I know the one who sits by his fire outside, why is he here? What man keeps him here as though his very life was being stolen away by a man. A white man?" The chief spoke and looked at Nadine who was pouring another cup of hot coffee. Once again the sugar bowl was almost emptied by the chief as he plied the sugar to his coffee.

"We don't know much about the man he was chasing through the scrub, but he ran up to the stock room where I was and fell at my feet. His throat was cut, not bad enough to kill him but deep enough to make him bleed out if he hadn't found us in time," Maude Elsie told the old Indian. Then took the coffee cup and filled it again for the Chief.

"Know that Indian man by the fire, he been at my main camp at creek when white man and Indian woman came to camp. Indian man like have woman. Like have woman from all womans." Chief Bow Legs said as he added sugar to his hot coffee. "Got coffee for Indian mans out side? They no use sweet. Only Chief get to drink sweet coffee," the Chief told Nadine who was heading out the kitchen door, and headed to the Indians sitting around the other Indian who had been there for days now. She handed each Indian a brand new shining tin cup and then picked up the two gallon pot and started pouring hot coffee to each man. The last to get his coffee was the Indian who tried to cut Harold's throat. They all drank the coffee and as Nadine started to walk off she sat the coffee pot near the fire to keep it hot for the men.

The next morning Chief Billy Bow Legs sent two men to the camp where the Indian tried to cut Harold's throat to bring back the woman in question. They were gone about five hours and as they arrived the woman would not look at the Indian man except to first glance recognition. She went directly to Harold and they were together again their child came running to the two and as far as Billy Bow Legs was concerned, that, was that. "You not good Indian man," he said to the Indian that tried to kill Harold, "You Tocca dik ne ne, and that will be your name from now on forever you will be known as snake belly, you no longer will hunt with my people you be no more in good with my tribe and all Seminole, now YOU GO_" the chief told the Indian and he walked into the scrub totally unarmed he didn't even get his knife back.

The sun rose again in the East and started another Thursday at the depot and general store. The smell of lye soap would soon permeate the rooms, kitchen, and dining room as it was the day to clean the depot and the general store.

Spurgeon had rounded up their three sons and two hands to saddle up and head into the scrub hunting for cows. That left the women alone to get the cleaning done in the buildings.

The women were dusting, sweeping, and moping the floors as they chatted and laughed at the past days activities, when Nadine asked Savannah, "Where is the Indian girl and the child, weren't they to stay here until Harold was able to move around again?" Savannah went to the door to look out into the dooryard to see if she could see the Indian woman and her little girl. She turned to tell Savannah, "that she could not see them in the yard." She turned around and the Indian woman was standing in the kitchen door. surprised Savanna shrieked for she was not expecting her to be there. The little girl was tugging at her Seminole dress and jumped when Savannah shrieked and the child's dark eyes got very wide as she was not sure why the scream. Then Savannah laughing grabbed them both in a hug and they all enjoyed the happy repast with a new friend.

"Where were you dear?" Maude Elsie asked.

"Bring wood to box, put water in buck for house, what more you want Fawn to do?" The Indian woman said.

"Fawn," Maude Elsie repeated after she heard the Indian say her name for the first time. 'What a beautiful name for such a beautiful young woman," Maude Elsie continued, "and what is the child's name, Fawn?"

"Little Cloud," Fawn told the women as they went back to their duties.

"Fawn, Harold, and Little Cloud," Nadine added, "we have a new family to settle in before someone else gets them for their neighbors."

Fawn said, "Me and Harold marry in church, have Christian marry then Little Cloud come to our home. We go to Indian camp stay there four year and the bad man want Fawn but Fawn not want that man. Harold said, "Stay away_" very loud Indian man try to kill Harold so he run away to here. Now Indian man will not have home anymore because of him like me too much."

The three women had stopped working and were listening intently at the story Fawn was relating. And so it went for that whole day until it was time to cook supper for the men who were just coming through the scrub, as the sun began to set on the depot and store.

MORE WORK BECAUSE OF THE SCRUB

Along with the seven cows the men rounded up they killed two foxes and two coyotes in the scrub, their pelts are worth about five dollars apiece at the Bodow's store in Kissimmee. One of the cows horned another cow and had to be shot but the meat didn't go to waste. As soon as the men hit the home place they started a fire in the smoke house to cure the beef with hickory and oak wood smoke. While the fire was getting ready they skinned the meat out and put the hide in salt water to keep over night As soon as the smoke house was filled with the meat and the fire was banked for the night, they were called to supper.

The long table in the dining room was just about filled with Harold, Fawn and Little Cloud, along with the regular diners and the boarders. Everyone knew about the good food that Maude Elsie spread on a table was worth waiting for. As soon as dark falls the folks start getting ready for their nights rest. The boarders go into the parlor to listen to the piano, guitar, fiddle and recorder which Savannah plays. Some of the songs the people sing to, but mostly listen and hum along with the melody. Until tired bodies and eyes cause them to seek their bed to snuggle in for another nights rest.

The new day is Friday, this is the day that the beds are changed and the fresh clean sheets are the best part of going to bed on this Friday night. But there is a lot of day before that can be done and the people are in to rest.

The smoke house must be attended to and the fires kept going so there is a lot of oak and hickory to be brought up. Spurgeon had found a limb which had been broken off in a recent storm. He took his rope and chain with one of the mules to pull the limb back to the dooryard where it could be sawn into lengths for the stove and the smoke house. The sawing has started and two men have pitched in and started splitting the wood and piling it near the smoke house door. The smoke house fireplace is on the side of the building and has steel doors that shuts tight and allows the fire to smolder as the wood burns it creates charcoal and that is used to fire up the forge at the blacksmith's shop. If more air is let in, to cool the fire, the wood turns to ashes and can be used for making lye soap.

It is important to get a good smokey, dried layer on the outside of the meat to keep it from spoiling.

The men head back into the scrub early and leave the tending of the smoke house fire to the women this morning. About two hours of riding into the scrub and they hear cows lowing, a lot of them. They turn toward the sound and figure if they don't have a brand or notch on them that will be some kind of a good deal for the loss of the one yesterday didn't help the cattle business that Spurgeon was wanting for this drive.

Spring always helps the cattlemen and cowboys as the cows now have calves that they are very particular about and if you get a calf away from its mammy, she will come hunting it and her horns are well used for fighting for her young one. They are usually the one which bunch up in the scrub, they were known as nurseries or calf bunches, as they protect other cows calves. The calves are normally in the center and lie down so the cows can graze around the bunch. That is what Spurgeon was hoping for today as they rode toward the bunch they could hear over in the scrub a ways. Right now the palmettoes were too thick and high to see what it was but they kept on heading in that general direction.

There they are_ Just circling the calves there were almost twenty five cows and calves in the nursery bunch, as they stirred the cowboys looked for marks or brands and when they saw no marks they slowly drifted and circled with the cows just out side the circling bunch. They would move in closer until they could be sure they would head toward the direction of the depot and the cow pens. As they got in with the herd they began cracking their whips and this started a mini stampede until the cows realized that their calves weren't with them then they would circle back to find their calf, this little exercise took the fight out of the cows and when they were paired up to their own calf, which took several hours, then for some reason they would let themselves be driven along the trail. The cowboys picked up several more scrub cows on the way and would wait to count at the Cowpens.

Jake Owen and Ski Shalen, were working the west side of the herd when they saw a kit fox in the trail. Jake pulled up his horse and found three more in the brush. He picked them up and put them in a burlap sack and hung them from his saddle horn. They whined and he knew that they were hungry and if they would last till they got to the depot then one of the women would adopt the kits and see that they were fed and kept warm. Jake took a lot of razzing from Ski on the drive to the depot but he was good for it and told how he would sell the kits to some unsuspecting Yankee, and make a few buck on the side. That didn't sway Ski though so he kept the persecution going until that evening at supper.

The last cow and calf were driven into the cowpen and Spurgeon counted thirty nine cows and calves. Then he checked to see that there was still enough firewood for the smoke house. The men filed toward the wash stand out beside the kitchen door which led into a mud room and into the kitchen, or turn left and you were in the dining room. The long tables were set and holding ready for the men to come in and eat the meal that was prepared by Maude Elsie, Savannah, and Nadine. Fawn was trying to help but she was still too week from the home sickness she came down with.

The men ate their meal and as they left the dining room they placed their dishes in the tub beside the door, and went outside to tend to their horses and bed them all down for the night. Thats when Jake remembered the kit foxes he had in the bag. He took the bag up to the kitchen door and called for Fawn to come to the door, when she came he handed her the bag with the four kits and said, "Their hungry we killed the vixen yesterday." Fawn took the small charges and placed them in a box that shotgun shells had been shipped in. Soon she was feeding them a little at a time. When they got their little bellies full of milk sweetened with sugar she found a quart jar which she filled with warm water and placed an alarm clock in the small nursery. As the little foxes huddled together they slept for a few hours then it was time to feed them again and this is what it took to get the homesickness out of Fawn. Cloud was a great helper the next day as the kits had to be fed every four hours day and night. Harold enjoyed the kits too and would time the banking of the smoke house fire to the feeding of the kits. The small charges took charge of the Richards family for a few weeks.

The cattle seemed restless and Jake Owen, the night rider just kept singing to them and trying to soothe them as best he could. He noticed that they would shy away from the fence in one particular section of the split rail pen. Jake carefully got down from his horse and went on foot to see what was happening in that side of the pen. As he eased up on the rail fence he saw that the two bottom rails were missing. He eased back to his horse got his rifle and bull whip, just in case he ran up on a person who was bent on cow stealing. He looked at the fence and as he did in the moonlight he saw the shadow of a man driving the small calves from the pen. The shadowy figure was having trouble keeping two of the calves moving and as one ran back to its mammy he kept the other moving toward the hole in the rail fence. The shadow drove the calf out of the pen and crawled out of the hole behind it.

Before he could stand up Jake's well placed rifle butt caught the back of the mans head and he dropped like a wet rag. Jake cracked his whip three times in succession and this brought the entire house and bunk house to the pens. Spurgeon had a lantern and Nadine had a coal oil lamp. They turned the man over and saw that it was the Indian man who Chief Billy Bow Legs had cast out of the tribe. He groaned and started to get up but fell back to the ground and did not move again.

"What you wont us'ens ta do wit ish here galoot mista Spurgeon?" Ski asked.

"Well we caint put en inta tha smoke house, I guess we'uns is got ta tie em up in tha barn," Spurgeon told the men.

They half drug and he half walked to the barn, he was tied to a column where he could not sit and had to stand on his feet till the morning came.

They quickly hustled the three small calves back into the pen and fixed the rails in the fence then went to the kitchen where Maude Elsie, Savannah, and Nadine had made coffee and there was some cake and pie left over from supper. This took the edge from the nerves of the Indian's captors and let them get back to sleep easier.

"I thank I aint gonna let Jake be no night rider no mo. He alus gits us up in the middle of the night to do hissen fighten fer him," Spurgeon teased Jake. The men and women laughed then they filed one by one back to their respective beds.

A NEST IN THE SCRUB

Maude Elsie and Savannah noticed that Nadine was conspicuous by her absence, even though they heard the scraping of furniture on the pine wood floor in her room; Nadine had not come out this morning even to get a cup of coffee or to eat breakfast. There was the sound again.

"What on earth is she doing in her room this morning?" Savannah asked, no one in particular, for it was a muse more than a question anyhow.

"I am sure I don't know what she is doing in there, I think she has moved every stick of furniture in her room except the bed. I guess she would move that too if it didn't weigh so much." Maude Elsie answered Savannah the same way the question was asked. Then she looked up at Savannah and smiled a Mona Lisa smile which hardly broke her lips. Then she said, "We better get to boiling some water around here. Nadine is about to have her babies_" The tone of the kitchen and the other ladies there created a movement of the ladies in the house and the daily chores were put on hold for the moment.

Nadine had just pulled the quilt spread from the bed when the small nagging pain in her back became a ripping, tearing pain coming from somewhere inside her stomachs. "That was one," she said to herself as she continued to pull the quilt from the bed. She folded it neatly and placed the folded quilt on the cedar chest at the foot of the bed. The next pain started in the small of her back and went down both legs, that caused her knees to buckle. Nadine tried to get up from the kneeling position she found herself in but she could not stand or even get one leg in front so that she could pull up on the post at the foot of the bed.

Another pain was coming this time from between her thighs as if she had a cramp and could not do anything about it.

"MAUDE ELSIE! . . . SAVANNAH! . . . ANYONE . . ., please help me I can't get up. Please help me I think the baby is coming." Nadine screamed as she fell to the floor.

Savannah was the first in the room, followed by Spurgeon and Claude Hayman. Claude swept Nadine up in his arms as Spurgeon turned the bed clothes back and Maude Elsie rushed into the room with a basin of hot water, towels and a oil cloth, table cloth to put under her before her water broke and soaked the linens and mattress. After the oil cloth was placed under Nadine the men left the room as Maude Elsie started undressing Nadine. Savannah stood watch over the patient and handed Maude Elsie a nightgown from Nadine's dresser drawer.

Nadine's water broke and there was what seemed to be gallons of pink liquid that Savannah channeled to the chamber pot and as the fluid stopped coming, towels were placed under Nadine as she was now in hard labor and the theme was, "breathe, push, and hold still,"

No one was ready when the first baby came into the world, but it slid out of the birth canal as though there was nothing to being born. Now with a quick squeak Maude Elsie took up the child as Savannah placed a clothespin on the umbilical cord, gave it a twist then cut the cord with scissors.

Nadine gave a hard push and the next baby's head exited the birth canal, one more push and Savannah had the baby wrapped in a towel and handed the baby to Maude Elsie. Maude Elsie called for Dixie and Birdie to come into the room to help. Birdie was just inside the room when the third baby slipped into the world and Savannah told everyone that, "She had better stop having babies pretty soon . . . I am running out of clothespin." they all laughed and even Nadine laughed but now she had had the last of the triplets, who were the first to be born in the scrub.

Nadine asked Maude Elsie, "What are they?"

"They are fine healthy human beings," Maude Elsie answered.

"Well . . . you know what I mean." Nadine begged.

"You have two little boys and one little girl. You have your work cut out for you, you must name them and you must figure out a feeding schedule since you have three young'uns but only two . . ." Savannah told Nadine over the crying of three healthy babies.

"Nadine, if you should not produce enough milk for the three babies we can get the Indian woman Tomega she is a wet nurse for the Indian mothers and she will help us out if you need her." Maude Elsie told Nadine.

The three babies were washed and cleaned and fed to the extent that Nadine could produce for the babies. And a baby in each arm and one on her tummy Nadine bonded to the babies as she sang a song to them, then drifted off to sleep.

Savannah and Maude Elsie took the babies and placed them in the crib that Brittinany and Davy Pearce gave to Nadine only a week ago. They saw how big Nadine had become with the full term babies.

The men all tried to look in on the new family but were shooed away until Nadine had some rest after her ordeal of the morning.

Spurgeon had gone to the corral and hitched up the buck board, to go into the Indian camp to find Tomega and bring her back to the depot. He took with him some blankets and a few yards of cloth the Indians would make shirts and dresses out of. He took a new hunting knife and a jug of wiskey. He knew that Tomega's brave would like to have her around but he would like the white mans plunder better. Spurgeon knew that there would possibly be a child that Tomega was still feeding and if possible he would bring that baby and its mother along with them too.

There was just such an action but the Indian mother said to, "go I will take care of the baby and perhaps wean him now."

It took most of a day but around four o'clock in the afternoon, Spurgeon came driving the buckboard and Tomega sitting on the back seat with her trappings loaded on behind her rode up to the depot door like the queen of Sheeba.

Tomega strode into the lobby of the depot boarding house and asked, "Where woman with babies?" She was led into the room where Nadine was just feeding two of the babies and the other was crying in the crib. Soon it too was hushed by the warm flow of mothers milk going to its growing belly.

Claude was the obedient servant of Nadine's and she only had to ask and if it were within his ability or grasp he would serve her. His ability to change the soiled diaper of one of the children was more than he could handle but it seemed that Tomega knew when a diaper was dirty and would change the baby's diaper. She would bathe them and Nadine, then she would go out and get Claude and bring him in to Nadine.

On a Sunday morning Claude hitched up the Western Union utility wagon and headed east on the Bent Penny Trace. He was gone until well past dark and Nadine along with the rest of the folks at the Depot Boarding house had begun to worry about him and if he had run into some type of problem in the eight mile trek to the Bent Penny Ranch. They knew that he had gone there because he left a message that he would return tonight and now it was night and if they don't hear from him with in the next hour or two Ski and one other would ride the Trace to see if he had broken down.

But their worries were foundless as around the ten o'clock hour the wagon rumbbled up into the dooryard and Claude hopped down and went to the tail gate and let it down. Then he led a nanny goat and in tow were two kids, about two months old. He led the nanny into the closed stall in the barn, gave her some grain and pitched her an abundance of hay for a bed and walked into the dining room. He asked if he could go in and see about Nadine and the children and of course it was alright. He picked Nadine's head up from the pillow and kissed her. She responded with a kiss and told him, "I missed you today."

"Did you have to do a repair?" Nadine asked as Claude laid her head back on the pillow.

"No, I had to make a trip to the Bent Penny Ranch, where I bought a nanny goat so the triplets can have enough milk to keep their little bellies full. I had been thinking about getting another cow but I don't know how to milk so I went to the best authority I know, Mary Remmick, she told me to get a goat and Tom and Blossom had so many they just up and sold me a nanny and the two kids went along with the bargain." Claude expounded.

"A goat_" Nadine said as she laughed, then added, "If you cant milk a cow how can you milk a goat?" then she laughed again, but this time she held her stomachs. "Ooo, Claude don't make me laugh it still hurts . . . but its a good hurt. I love you and your kind ways, I don't know what I would do without you, my dearest Claude."

"Well first of all I took lessons in milking from Tom and Blossom, they would not let me load up the goats until I had mastered the chore and I only have one bruise from the first kick she gave me; I suppose that my hands were too cold to suit her nibs, so she blasted me one with her right hind leg, she kicked me so fast all I felt was the pain and she didn't even kick the milk pail," Claude quipped. He added, "As far as doing without me you had better get used to having me around cause you and I are gonna git hitched when you get well and up and around on your all two's, dear lady."

"Sir is that a proposal to marriage?" Nadine smiled as she asked.

"If it isn't its the closest I know how to make one," Claude teased.

"You would feel awful funny if I accepted wouldn't you?" said Nadine.

"Yes; would be the golden word that I would want to hear," Claude said as he looked deeply into Nadine's eyes and a plea shown in his eyes as he hesitated waiting for her answer.

Nadine sighed, glanced over at the crib which held her three week old babies and without looking back at Claude, she said, "Yes."

Claude went into the telegraph office and tapped on the key, "Congratulate me! I'm going to get married and become a father_" then signed off, "Claude."

With the advent of the nanny goat Tomega knew that she would not be needed anymore and as she packed her belongings she ask Nadine, "Tomega, love little Nadines, like come back see some more, please."

Nadine was now up and around somewhat, so she grabbed Tomega and gave her a great big hug and patted her on the back which Tomega returned for it meant in Seminole they were great friends and welcome always where ever they met.

Tomega went to the triplets and changed their diapers for a last time, took up her bundle and disappeared into the scrub.

"Good by, my dear friend," Nadine said tearfully as she watched Tomega walk into the scrub toward her family of Seminoles camped near the Depot Boarding House and General Store.

The sun was going down into the scrub and the babies were hungry and needed changing, Nadine started in with the little girl, then the two boys and that chore was done, but there was the hunger, and would not be satisfied without nourishment. The goat's milk served one while Nadine served the other two. This system was changed every day as each child would get the mothers milk for three days and the goat's milk one day, until one day the triplets kept crying and fussing until Maude Elsie told Nadine that, "they are hungry, and if you don't have enough milk then you best get started on the goat's milk between your breast feedings.

Three bottles of goat's milk was produced and the triplets ate with a passion, giving small squeaks and gulping sounds as they drained the bottles, then they slept for another four hours into the night.

Thinking ahead there were three more bottles set and ready in the ice box for the next feeding time in the Depot Boarding House and General Store.

14

A Bee Tree In The Scrub

With the awakening of Spring there was an aroma in the air of blossoms, blooms, buds and Honey Suckel, to be enjoyed by any human who would notice. The only drawback was that next followed the rain, to the point where people of the scrub would like to see some sunshine and had limited bouts of cabin fever. But now was the time to enjoy the smell of the blooms in the air and should be pleasing to everyone.

The triplets were going on three months now and were all on goats milk as Nadine had found that she was not producing breast milk at all now. It didn't seem to make any difference as the babies were still healthy and had not so much as had a cold since they were born. Sarah had a greater propensity for food than the boys. She would drink from her bottle and eat the soft food from the table. The boys wanted the bottles and were merely passive about the other food. Never-the-less they were hearty and could be heard all the way to the barn. There was hardly any place to go that would give a body peace and quiet so one might just as well let it go and keep the dry, clean diapers coming.

Nadine was back to her gourmet food served to the most appreciative diners in central Florida. Savannah was baking pies and cakes to please the pallets of the guests who came from all over to eat the food so wonderfully prepared by the caring hands of Nadine and Savannah. Maude Elsie still had a trick or two up her sleeve too. And would wow the people and their appetites for southern fried chicken, potato salad, mustard or turnip greens, black-eyed peas, fresh baked bread, and honey or jam to fill the edge of a sweet tooth and make the pleasure of eating so much more than being filled and leave. One must surly savor the aroma coming from the kitchen and still have to wait until all the diners could eat at the same time.

When Maude Elsie rang the dinner bell the rush was on and the answer to where did the "Boarding house reach," come from, the explanation would be there at that table in the Depot boarding house as it was like every man for himself. Grabbing, dipping, stabbing with a fork and sometimes passing on a dish as the meal progressed.

Large bowls of food were placed on the table to be passed and shared and if a bowl was emptied then another was set in its place. The meat platters were the same and it seemed that they were always the first to be cleaned by the hungry folks at the dining tables. Fresh melons were offered from the farm, as well as strawberries and if someone would pick them fresh blackberries with cream. Dessert would bring delicious pecan pies, strawberry pie or strawberry short cake with whipped cream, and often Savannah would bake several layer cakes with chocolate icing.

Everyone just longed for the wonderful food that was put on to that table and at Christmas the tables were complete with festive fair of home-cured hams, wild turkeys, roast beef, fried chicken, and then there was the stuffing, honey sauce, cream gravy, and the wonderful pies and cakes, and the homemade candies.

Leftovers were as welcome as the original courses and when the holiday meal was finished and the dishes washed and put away the women would look at the men with their belts let out a notch or two and dozing in chairs in the parlor, porch swing and porch floor. The women went into the sewing room and then the gossip flew as the wings of a shot at quail, but they never missed their shot of talk and it was always about someone or something that wasn't there. They worked on quilts, crochet throws, dresses, and even shirts for the men. There was the buckskin that was ready to be made into jackets, shoes and pulled lacings for the shoes and jackets. When the loom was operated and there was flay to weave the shuttle made its rhythmic thump and the women kept talking in time with the thumping of the shuttle and laughed and cried from telling funny stories, or sad ones. And always the children were the main topic of their conversation. Now they had the triplets to go on about and the mounds of diapers they had and will create. On and on they went until they automatically started for the kitchen and the tasks were to do over again as it was said women's work is never done. Supper was easier for they all got warmed overs, which is the same as they got at dinner.

The telegraph started clacking in the Western Union office and Claude went to hear what was so important on this spring day.

It was the Bent Penny Ranch wanting to know if Doc Zimmerman was at the depot or if anyone knows where he is. They have had a man hurt and need the doctor.

The doctor was there eating the noon meal then he left and was traveling east on the Bent Penny Trace, the last anyone saw of him. Spurgeon sent Jake Owen and Norm Tracy on horse back to try to catch up with the doctor. Then go all the way to the Bent Penny Ranch and see if they can help in any way.

The two men left shortly before two o'clock and went at a fast trot, when Spurgeon cracked his whip three times. They turned the horses and Spurgeon said, "You run them horses and whut ah'm a sayin is if they drop then git a'tuther an run him too!" the two turned and spurred up the horses to a fast run, and soon disappeared into the scrub. After running for about twenty minutes the two saw a buggy up ahead and started cracking their whips three times then stop and then crack them three more times. The buggy stopped and a man got out but it didn't look like the doctor. The man waited until the cowboys caught up then they realized the doctor was not wearing his suit and tie and then they greeted him and said, "A man was hurt at the Bent Penny Ranch and they sent a wire asking for you to come there and see about him."

The doctor stepped back into his buggy and whipped his horses up to get to the ranch as soon as he could, while the two went along to give any assistance they could.

They arrived about dusk and the men met the doctor, Jake and Owen as they came in the gate at the Bent Penny Ranch. They brought the doctor into the guest room at the house and as he walked in with his little black bag in hand the doctor asked, "What's the trouble here?"

"We'uns found a bee tree over in the scrub and young Billy here stood up on the back o hissen's Marsh Tackie but he caint rech hit no how, so he's a try'n ta shinny up at aire bee tree when tha bees done fine hima shinny'n on their tree. Them bee critter done commenced ta sting at aire boy an he come down frum at aire tree, but he done brung them there bees wid'm when them little ole bee critter done bit on the Marsh Tackie, hit tooken off from that there place and hid in the scrub some. But Billy was a comin from up at aire tree and he just had ta slide some. He got splinners an bee stings and we brung him ta tha house with him a yellen and talkin bout how he gonna cut at aire tree down and them bees wont got no home no more. I rec'con they's muss be bout fifty poundses o honey comb in at aire tree, I rec'con, doan cha know.

Miz Mary done put soady on them bee whelps and pine gum salve on the splinter holes on his'ens lags and arms whur he helt onto at aire tree acommin down," Jeremiah told the doctor as they walked together to little Billy's bedside.

"Hiz daddy Tom iza riden patrol and wont be back to this here side of the scrub fer bout fo ares yet now," Earl Ray said as he stuck his head in the door to see if anything had changed.

"Blossom, yall wonts me ta sen affer Tom and let him know in son is a ailin?" Jeremiah asked Billy's mother.

"No sir, just let the doctor look at him first then if the doctor thinks we should get Tom we will decide then if Tom is back by that time," Blossom answered.

"Ok then we'uns'll wait fer tha doc ta say," Jeremiah told Blossom.

"Get a pan of water and wash this stuff off the boy so I can see what is wrong and how to fix it," the doctor said.

Blossom literally ran to the kitchen and got a large pan of hot water and a bottle of turpentine to use as a base to remove the pine gum salve.

Soon the boy was free of his baking soda and pine gum and the doctor set in to get the splinters out of the young lad. The more he pulled from the kid the more the kid hated that bee tree. It was dark and supper was ready by the time the doctor had all the splinters out and the wounds closed, some of them needed a stitch or two but the lad did not yell or scream but the bee tree was in dire peril.

It seemed that in spite of all the wounds, stings and stitches the appetite of young Billy was not daunted. He ate a Herculean amount of food and drank two glasses of milk and ate a large piece of chocolate cake.

"Why are you eating and drinking so much tonight, Billy?" his mother asked.

"I've got to grow big and strong so that I can cut down that bee tree, eat all of their honey, and kill all of the bees. For this I must be big, strong, brave and use the hate I have in my soul to be done with that bee tree and all of the bees in it." Billy replied.

"Why do you harbor so much hate in your soul?" Mary asked.

"Have you seen the wounds that my body has and the stitches . . .?" Blossom put her hand over little Billy's mouth and hushed him lest he says something that his seven year old soul may not justify if he is called to his maker, Blossom figured that the embarrassment now would be better than to stand before the Lord and explain to him how his hate might cause him to not get into Heaven.

"Mother can you stand to see my body scarred and stung and not let me get the satisfaction of getting even?" Billy had removed his mothers hand and began to explain his wrath.

"Vengeance is mine, I will repay, saith the Lord," Blossom told Billy and then she leaned over and whispered something in his ear, at which time Billy looked at her and said excuse me and ran out of the dining room and into the office.

The supper was finished without anymore excitement and the men went to the porch to smoke and await the coffee call which would be after the ladies had finished with the dishes and the men were to meet and have coffee and dessert if they wanted but the main reason for the coffee time was to plan the next day's work. This way the ones who had the patrol would know what to do when they woke up after their day sleep and finish the day with the balance of the crew.

Mary and little Mary were on the way to the cabin when little Billy rushed by sobbing and went to the cabin and slammed the door behind him.

Blossom and Tom walked by and spoke to Mary and Little Mary said "Billy's mad and I'm glad, and I know what will please him . . ." Blossom glanced over her shoulder and said, "Hush Mary, don't you start too."

Billy did not get the licking he thought he would but went to bed with a pretty good grouch on still and was soon asleep.

Tom looked in on the children and found that little Billy was not in his bed. He had gone through his window and to the stable put the bridal on his Tacky and ridden off into the night.

Blossom went to the house and told the men, as soon as they could they saddled up and Tom said, "I think I know where he went, he mos lackly been a goin ta tha bee tree."

Blossom went to the kitchen and started making coffee and sandwiches for the men to have a snack when they came back in later. She shook to think what she would do to, "little Billy's behind if he were here right now." but then she knew that she would not because she had the chance earlier and only talked to him. Thats when he ran from the office to the cabin.

Billy was indeed at the bee tree and had his little axe and was chopping away at the tree when the men came up.

"Its a good thang hits dark time and them bees is a asleepin some cuz he would be a stinging lack they haint never afore been a stingin nobody a fore" Jeremiah said as he reached down from his saddle and picked up Billy by the scruff of the neck. When he did Billy just hung there like a little kitten being moved by its mother. Jeremiah handed Billy to Tom and Tom took him to his Tacky and put him on it and said, "NOW RIDE YOUNG MAN,"

The party came again into the yard and John Henry Luke took the horses to the barn and unsaddled them and gave them a quick brushing and some oats and let them back into the corral.

From that night forward that bee tree was off limits except once a year when it was robbed of its honey and honey comb. It became another tree in the scrub.

The next morning Norm and Jake headed for home and the depot to find the ladies again ironing and folding the clothes as another week had already started and the women had it all to do over again.

FLOUR, LARD AND SOME LITTLE MILK

Wednesday, the day for baking and the flour was showing moisture as the summer seemed to never end this year. The rains of May, June, July and now August were still causing the creeks to run over their banks and the Peace Creek was nearly into Bartow as it continued to swell. Most of the water was not very deep only about to a horses ankle but it was causing the problem of the horses and cattle to have infections and yeast mold in the hooves of the animals. There was only one place to move them to and that was the sand ridge over around the Bent Penny Ranch, but even they were finding it more and more difficult to locate higher ground for their livestock. Never-the-less Jeremiah had Davy wire over to the Tanners to see if they wanted to drive their stock over to the ridge. Spurgeon quickly accepted and began to round up the men to let them know of the drive to the Bent Penny Ranch.

"Chandler Owen, Shalen Brokowski, and Norm Tracy, I wont you three ta gote tha pasture an git them cow critters an herd 'em up ta tha Trace here, Maude Elsie and the lady folk is a gonna git sum grub up fer ya ta take wiff ya. So stop here an let me talk ta ya sum more afore ya git to herd'n up the Trace," Spurgeon told the men, as he assigned the jobs to all of the hands, men and women.

"Dixie and Birdy will make a chuck wagon and the team will be the Music team,(that is what the team had been nick named that belonged to the professor) they are more dependable and easier for the women to handle." Maude Elsie told the group, then went back into the kitchen.

The water was now up to the hubs on the chuck wagon and the ox carts were used for the hands to transport their duffel. These carts were higher and most likely to keep the belongings out of the water. The rain was still coming down and at least sometime during the day it would rain. The pioneers wondered if there was a hurricane coming but there was never any wind to speak of, so it wasn't like a storm was coming, just the rain and so much of it when it rained.

Kissimmee River was flooding and taking up a lot of flat lands too the cattle and the horses and other live stock, goats and sheep came toward the highlands of the area around Lake Wailes and on the Florida Ridge. The town of Kissimmee was inundated by the river flowing over its banks a half mile away. Therefore any place which had no standing water was being used by some type of livestock, and more often a mixture of all kinds of creatures.

Steam boats on the Kissimmee River were having problems of staying inside the channel, and the flowing water was carrying the sand bars and placing them in unlikely places for a sandbar, causing the steamboats to run aground often while steaming up or down the Kissimmee River. Some of the shallow draft paddle wheelers were able to sail up to the courthouse in Kissimmee. One man caught a large catfish while standing on the courthouse steps in the middle of town.

The truck crops were wiped out all along the flat land away from the ridge. Some of the farmers and ranchers that had bees would put the hives and supers on barrels to keep the bees from drowning. The rain was causing a lot of problems for all of Central Florida and unless it stopped sometime soon the cattle industry will be finished in this area too.

People were now moving their livestock toward the east and would soon be using the Trace for their movement also. Spurgeon wired Jeremiah at the Bent Penny and told them the problem they were facing as the Trace got more and more traffic on it in the form of people, wagons, ox carts, and animals. Jeremiah wired back saying, "take your animals and beings to the south for about two miles and follow the old cattle trail from Blue Forest to the backbone and keep going east till you reach the old Indian seedling grove and stop and make your camp there for there is a spring well that flows and there will be plenty of good sweet water you can rely on."

Spurgeon and Maude Elsie packed their duffel and placed it on the chuck wagon and with a whistle and a whip crack the people and the herd turned south from the Trace and waded through the water for two miles where they found a long mound that was indeed above the waterline and the cattle and dogs headed for it instinctively, the mules and horses pulled and carried the people in the wagons upon the rise and they stayed there until the water receded almost a month and a half later.

The seedling grove was about thirty or fourty seedling orange trees with one rough lemon and two grapefruit trees. The fruit on the orange trees were sweet and the oranges were squeezed and much orange juice was enjoyed, as long as the young boys were able to climb the trees to get to the fruit, for these trees were more than thirty feet tall. There were no ladders that tall so the campers had to rely on the young men to climb and throw the oranges to someone on the ground. The lemon tree could be picked from the ground, now too with as many seeds as there were the grove would surely expand at some point.

The women worked well together and Maude Elsie said, "Even though we are out in the open and living in tents the food is still fit for a king. Because of the triplets and little Cloud the milk cows and goats were kept like they were royalty, on the trek out here the goats rode inside the wagon and now here they are under a tent along with the milk cows and there has never been anything like this that I know of."

The cook tent was like being at home, there was the large wood burning stove with its stovepipe running outside and up a few feet to exhaust with a good draw to make the fire hotter and the wood burn more efficiently. The stove's appetite for wood was becoming a problem as there was a lot of forest on the backbone but the trees were large pine and hard to cut with saw and axe and even harder to split, but since there were very few chores for the men to do around the cattle they could split wood for the fires and keep the kitchen stove hot.

The heat from the stove in the kitchen tent was welcome as the rain kept everything wet or damp from the humidity. Therefore every chance the men would take as they passed by the kitchen would back up to the stove and get kind of warn and dry for a few minutes any how.

Now that the folks from the Bent Penny were with the group of Tanner's there were a lot more mouths to feed and even the Seminoles were wandering onto the backbone now. The Chief Billy Bow Legs mostly sat in the kitchen tent near the stove, Mary and Maude Elsie put him a small table there so he could hear the conversation and when he wanted coffee he would simply ask and one of the women would pour him a cup of coffee. He would take care of the sugar with always six to eight spoons full into the cup and drink it so hot a white person could not stand coffee that hot. He had his own cooks with him and his braves would hunt the woods near by and always bring one or two dear to the camp.

The Chief had the braves make a fire ring and the large Indian woman who cooked for the Chief mostly would always make some type of bread for him and would toss it between her hands with a pat, pat, pat, back and forth until she felt it was the correct shape and thickness. Then she would spit on the flat stone and if the spittle danced across the hot flat stone she would toss the bread on the stone and sing an Indian song and when she came to the part of the song where she grunted she would grasp one edge of the bread and flip it over and begin to sing to it again. The next grunt the bread would be a golden brown on each side then it was placed on a plate with a meat and a vegetable then placed before the Chief with a piping hot cup of coffee and he would eat the food slowly as his teeth were not so great anymore. The Chief, who was in his nineties now, often said that his teeth had eaten many deer and pulled many sinew for a bow string, but his teeth could still chew what he needed to eat and he still had his hunting knife to cut his meat a little smaller.

Savannah was the baker in the Tanner household and watched with her culinary curiosity as the old Indian woman made the bread for the Chief and the others in the Chief's camp and asked her if she would give her the receipt for the bread.

"You take flour, you take lard, and some little milk and mix it together and you pat it in hands then when you spit on stone and it do the war dance across it then it hot for bread. I sing it song of wonderful days it will have in pleasing the great chief and when come to end make like chief and grunt. Bread ready turn over, sing song again when grunt last time bread cooked, give to my Chief, and he grunt," The old woman looked at Savannah and they both laughed at the cute story that came with the Indian bread receipt. The old woman added, "for birthday I put sugar in bread for my Chief, he like that much." It took many hours of trying before Savannah mastered the technique, she also found the bread tasted differently if she did not spit on the griddle to see if it was hot enough.

One morning the sun was out and the humidity was almost to the dripping off the ceiling point. The cows and horses would wade out into the water to get out of the heat. The goats would watch from the safety of their wagon. In just about as much time as it took to get everything packed for the trip to the backbone it was dry enough to return to the different homes. Nadine was anxious to see Claude and of course Brittany was looking forward to see Davy, the two stayed at the telegraph keys making sure there was no hurricanes coming and they had to eat their own cooking for a month and a half. Most of the men were wondering what the flood was all about and were anxious to ask Davy or Claude about the past weather.

Claude told the story, "The ships had reported two hurricanes one in the gulf and one south of Key West and since the high pressure stayed over Savannah, Georgia it kept the two hurricanes at bay until one turned and went into Texas, the other went out into the Atlantic. But it surely messed up the atmosphere in our area, they were talking about a little under fifty inches of rain in the last two months."

The wood stove was last to be moved and with the different pieces coming apart with stove bolts and in some cases baling wire kept the stove together and without them it came apart very easy. However it did take up a wagon load all by itself and as the wagon load of stove went down the trail to the Bent Penny Ranch, Jake Owen noticed the grass crunching under the wagon wheels. This seemed strange since they just went through fifty inches of rain but the crunch of the grass made him afraid of wild fires in the scrub. He asked himself, "Why would the grass be so dry it looks like it would be so green and lush but no, somehow it got dead and now it will most likely cause the woods to burn again, dang . . . I hope not . . . not again."

And indeed when they got home and unpacked Spurgeon and Maude Elsie gave the same warning, "The grass is not lush and green so that there will be a present danger of fire. Now each person here is responsible to each other to keep the fire danger down and be careful of the lit cigarettes, matches and campfires. Maude Elsie spoke to the men while they were eating. Then Spurgeon took the floor and said, "Ever thang whut Maude Elsie done said is the gospel an you better heed her words. Now Mr.

Jeremiah Coxin, over to tha Bent Penny is done toll us'ens we kin borry their John Deere plow and eight up mules ta plow us a far gard round this here place so if'n hit come a far hit wont lackly jump that there far gard an come in ta tha depot and gen'al stoe. Until the new grass is done growed out we'uns is got ta make our'n home as far proof as we'uns kin."

The dogs started to bark and they heard the whistle of a mule in the Trace and when they looked out they saw John Henry Luke with the huge John Deere plow and with the eight mule team pulling it would take down small saplings and cypress knees. The plow shears gleamed in the bright sunlight and the green and yellow paint made the implement look like a circus wagon for some reason, perhaps the bright colors of the plow.

Spurgeon saddled up his Marsh Tacky and headed down the lane beside the general store then backdown the lane and around the bay head, then east to the creek where they stopped and ate lunch. Then on north and back to the Bent Penny Trace. John Henry went to the kitchen and asked for a glass of water then after taking care of his thirst asked if, "Mr. Spurgeon was still about?"

Spurgeon walked into the kitchen and asked, "Did you want me, John Henry?"

"Yessir, I jist wants ta know If'n yall wants me ta plow 'nother hedge round your property?" John Henry asked.

Spurgeon said, "Yes John Henry, but that is Bent Penny land you don't thank that Mr. Coxin or Mr. Remmick would want another cut lack that there in their woods?"

"Yes sir you see Mr. Remmick done said to make sure that thar far gard was a good'n so I don't mine a plowin a tuther un," John Henry said as he started out the door, he turned and asked, "Kin ah water them mule critters in your waterin' trough? Ah kin pump tha water awright."

Spurgeon told him, "You shouldn't ax me sumpin lack dat, why shore you'ens kin let them mules drank till we caint pump no mo."

The women had it the roughest for they had to clean all the mildew out of the house and a lot of lye water drained through the wooden floors of the depot and the general store. The dogs went to the barn to sleep and watch the dooryard because of the lye water under the porch. Even a barrel of salt had to be taken back to Davy to be reprocessed and sent back as good as new.

Some cows and horses had to be destroyed because of the infections in their hooves but none of the riding stock ever got the yeast infection in the hooves. The vet didn't know of any cure for the infection, so the animal had to be put down.

Little by little things got back to normal and the routine was broken occasionally by Savannah with her pat, pat, pat, patooie, and plop of her Indian bread and she made it as authentically as possible even spitting on the grill, but no one complained about the fine bread she was making now and again, "You take flour, you take lard, some little bit of milk . . ."

WHERE IS PAPA BOWLEGS

Little Billy, came riding up on his Marsh Tackie and dismounted in front of the general store. He took off his new Stetson hat and brushed the dust from it as he entered the store.

"Have you seen Papa Bowlegs?" he asked Claude as he walked past the Western Union window in the store.

"No, I haven't Billy. Isn't he in the camp?" Claude stated.

"No sir, he hasn't been home for several days now. I wonder if he is hunting somewhere," Billy said.

"Oh dear I hope he is not lost, he is past ninety now and I don't like to think about that poor ole soul being out in the scrub and not being able to get to help if he needed it," Maude Elsie said.

"He wouldn't be lost in the scrub, if that is where he is . . ." Billy trailed off as he looked toward the scrub and saw a strange light coming from the scrub. In all his twelve years Little Billy had never seen anything like it.

Little Billy, and Maude Elsie, looked at the strange blue light. They both started for the door and bolted outside to gather the reason for the strange light. As they reached the edge of the scrub they heard chanting and went slowly toward the singing. They rounded the side of the hammock and there sat the Chief, as big as life. He was singing and when the others sat down to ask what the chief was singing about.

Savannah looked at the old chief and knew that the song was his death song. She turned and ran back to the house and started heating the stone griddle which she had one of the Indians to make for her. She put together the Indian bread and plopped it on the griddle. While the bread was baking she made coffee and had it boiling hot as she put it into the glass jar to keep warm when wrapped in the sheep's wool. The coffee stayed hot for a long time and when she had the bread baked she ran back to the hammock to find the old chief lying down and making motions with his hands. He sat up for his meal of meat and bread that Savannah had created for him. He said something in his language, picked up the coffee, added six to eight spoons full of sugar and drank the liquid down. Maude Elsie poured him another and as he was spooning the sugar into the cup he dropped the spoon and slumped over.

Billy was the first to him with Spurgeon on his heels. Maude Elsie and Savannah felt for a pulse in his neck but the old warrior was now in his hunting grounds and the Indian women began to chant and shuffle their feet as though they would dance, but none of the Indian women stood up to dance they all sat very still except for their feet moving to the rhythm of the drum in the back ground.

Six braves stood, picked up the body of their chief and walked slowly into the scrub. The drums sounded for six days and on the seventh fell silent. And the scrub was so quiet that if a bird had chirped it would have sounded like a scream. Never has the scrub ever been that quiet.

The six braves reappeared from the scrub and went to the door of the depot and asked for food, for they had not eaten but only drank water for the six days of the chief's funeral. No one knew what had happened to the chief's body as it was placed on the top of a high platform of cypress poles, covered with palmetto fronds and his favorite blanket and there he was laid to rest.

Maude Elsie, Savannah and Nadine all pitched in and had food on the table in short order for the Indian braves. As they ate they were not the usual quiet peaceful men that they had been when the chief was with them. Now perhaps they thought the chief's spirit was not around them any more. They were wrong for when the women who had been drumming for them for the last six days came into the dining hall they became very quiet and peaceful again.

The women ate and drank as the men did but not at the same table, the women seemed to have a different conversation and it all hushed when a very imposing figure stepped inside the dining room.

The quiet was astonishing as the braves stood up and the women stood up to greet the new chief of the Seminoles.

"I am Chief Tallahassee. I will take all of the braves and women of this camp with me to the Saw Grass country, where you will join with the others who were of the Chipco tribe and followers, since Billy Bow Legs has gone his camp is without a chief. I shall be that chief from now on," the imposing figure said, and with this the Indians left the diningroom and entered the scrub.

Tallahassee, was indeed an imposing figure of a man who stood six feet and a little more. His dress was of the many colored pieces of cloth sewed together to give his shirt of cotton, linen and other bands of material a colorful finish in the shirt. The long sleeves were an exact match to each other and was carried across the body of the shirt, the stripes of many colors to make the shirt complete was a collar of silk and sewn beads and buttons to set the collar off as no one had ever seen before. His wild hair was a large tuft around his head and over his eyes to appear that he was glaring from under the fronds of a palmetto shrub. A half a dozen feathers from different exotic birds were stuck in no particular order around throughout his mane and for all looked like a peacock which had some of the regal feathers missing from its fan. The trousers the chief had on were from the woolen uniform trousers which the army wore during its campaign against the Seminole some seventy years hence. He wore white spats over his bare feet, but all in all cut quite a figure for the Indian women to eye, and the braves to follow but not let him make eye contact with them as they thought he could rob them of their soul.

Several weeks passed before there was any sight of the Indians in these parts and when the day came that they reappeared, the telegraph line was a buzz for the news of the Indians being back was indeed good news and somehow comforting too.

Gone however was the smile of Chief Billy Bow Legs and since there was hardly anything different about the Indians themselves there was less spirit in the women as they went into the general store and would touch things like cook pots, blankets, colored clothe, they would not trade; they simply looked then left the store.

Maude Elsie caught the old wet nurse and since they had many hours of talking while she was feeding one of Nadine's triplets, Maude Elsie thought she could talk to the woman and find out what was happening to the camp.

"On one week and one week we listened to the new chief then he wanted Seminole to go to Saw Grass River, we no boat people we must stay on our land and hunt, grow garden, make the things for trade. We no want go to Saw Grass River. We stay here on our land. We have big council fire and make decide we stay on our land, we make Tallahassee go back to Saw Grass River. Umph, we not make to go walking to river we like here buy, trade, we like it here, umph." the lady spoke with tears in her eyes and when Maude Elsie saw the tears she grabbed the woman and hugged her, and said, "You are not to go anywhere but you stay here and trade with us when you want something come to me."

"You good med'cin Maw Essie," the woman sobbed and turned to the kitchen, sat at the table and asked for coffee, she was served with a cup and the spirit of the chief still lived as she spooned six or eight spoons full of sugar into the coffee and stirred it well before she drank it.

Maude Elsie smiled as she counted the spoons of sugar to go into the cup. "At least she didn't drink it while it was still boiling as the Chief did," she muttered to herself as she set a wedge of pecan pie in front of the Indian woman and one more for herself with coffee.

The next morning there were fifteen to twenty Indians male and female waiting for the store to open at five a m, they had a lot to trade; smoked deer hides, smoked meats, deer, alligator, rabbit, fish and other things which would not agree to the white mans palate. They wanted the cook pots, blankets, knives, sugar, salt, bacon, flour, lard and now a little Orange Blossom perfume for the women to wear which was strictly taboo when the chief was alive. Each tried a little behind the ears and did a little sashay as she passed a brave in the store.

Maude Elsie looked at Spurgeon, and pressed her finger to her lips in the sign of "shhh." Spurgeon smiled and winked at his wife as they enjoyed the spirit of the people being back in the Indians again.

When the Tanners closed the store at six pm, they stood at the door of the kitchen and as Nadine poured them a cup of coffee and set a wedge of pecan pie in front of them they took it all in and said, "It is good to be back into familiar times again," then they all fell silent while thinking about their old friend Chief Billy Bow Legs and his camp of followers there in the scrub.

Though there were fewer Indians the next day the trading was the same for flour, lard, salt, cloth and for the brave a new knife.

There was no talk of any new chief in the camp as far as the whites knew they had no new chief, at least not one known to them, yet.

WHO IS THE CHIEF

The Indian way did not break down as far as naming a new chief was concerned. They simply picked the most brave of the braves. There was little political push or pull as far as the men are concerned. But, the Indian women that is to say the mothers of the braves who are in the running for chief will do just about anything to get her son elected chief. There would be dirty looks in the camp as one mother passed another. The friend of the mother would pressure the younger women to make sure they say something great in the chickee as they gathered for the night meal. They would pass the word at the spring or the communal baking oven, the horse pen and the cow pen had to be cleaned by the women. They made sure that a fledgling in the camp got the dirty jobs unless they agreed to speak to their father or another man in the camp about her mother's pick for chief, or she learned that if she married she would not ever again have to muck the corral after the cows and horses. They learned early and young what to do and what not to do when it comes to choosing a superior for the camp. Go with the majority, and not with your heart.

The women would be sure that the deciding vote got the best of everything a man could ask for. While the brave that was leaning toward a candidate other than his wife's best friend she would manage to make his meal less than palatable until he got the message.

Since the women could not vote on the chief, they had little to do with the outcome of the election of the chief the majority decided would be a good brave, then and only then would the meals return to the standard by which each individual woman was to give her all. Her husband might think he has done a wise and faithful job of electing a new chief the women knew who it was that decided those things. And the little darlings went about the camp as though they had nothing to do with the election of the new chief.

The politicking began on the eve of one of the Seminoles festivals and there was a lot of wrangling going on in the camp, for instance while working the melon field as they chopped a weed they would say the opponent's name, like a curse, for leaving the camp without permission.

Often the brave himself would not know that his name was in the pot, but his mother or wife knew and would have a few thoughts about doing all she knew to do for her man.

So, who is it going to be? Who will win the battle of the wills, the nudge of the elbow, the Winning way of the women, who would have their man for chief. Which man would come out on top. Who would become the new chief. Now don't forget it would be the bravest of the braves.

Much is being said about Leo Two Feathers, there is Tiger Two Cypress, Chill-ee-wa-ka, Toe-hope-ta-laga, Dancing Bear, Grinning Dog and Spec-ma-ta-ma. And all are married but for Leo Two Feathers, he is so, well, plain. He has straight hair, brown eyes with hardly any eye brow to create expression. His nose is far too large for his face and divides his eyes like a delta does two rivers. Leo Two Feathers is very tall well over six feet and his feet covers so much ground they say they could plant a garden in every foot print. His long bony arms are too long for his body and reach almost to his knees.

What is it that people see in such an example of a prospect for the duty of chief of the camp. It may be forgotten that Leo didn't have to swim the torrent of the rain swollen stream to save Doe Foot's five year old son from drowning, or perhaps they will remember it was he who found the bee tree that yielded so much honey they would have enough for the camp and still sell over one hundred dollars worth to the general store. How he cut fire wood for Maude Elsie and the other women when the men were cow hunting. He even found where the sacks of gold that were placed in the closet at the Bent Penny Ranch had caused the floor to give way to it's weight and fall under the house. Leo furnished the fish for the smoke house and the deer one year when the entire camp was sick with some type of influenza but no one died. Leo brought in the meat, and vegetables, water, milk for the babies and was the longest on the last scrub fire line, until it was out.

This strange looking but fine man who had nothing more than the welfare of the camp on his mind at anytime. Leo was head and shoulder, literally, above the others who would have their name mentioned at the council fire. But Leo had no idea that he was being considered. He simply went about his duties and assisting his people in the camp.

The council fires burned bright and long as the hours dragged into days and nights until there was hardly a brave on the council that wasn't so deprived of sleep that the thinking went crazy, and after the final draft and say so of the camp leader, the drums went silent. Those who were sleeping while the drums were drumming, awakened due to the silence. For a long five minutes the scrub was silent. The camp began to stir and soon every soul in the camp including the children were surrounding the council to see what was the outcome of the council.

Then with the shock of the longest time anyone could remember, the council announced that the new chief was none other than Leo Two Feathers. It was two o'clock in the morning by the time they got through celebrating and the camp settled in for the night.

Leo Two Feathers was the only one who could not sleep that night as he wondered why they had chosen him as their chief. Was this some type of cruel joke that the braves were playing on him or were they serious as to the outcome of the deciding nod. The pipe was lit and smoked as was the custom of the tribes even in the western world of the Indian. But for the fact that Leo Two Feathers was not at the council fires, he was attending an old man and woman who could no longer chew the meat that was brought, and had to be chewed by the women of the camp. Leo had the time and went to the chickee. He even brought good news that the council was about to choose another chief. Leo had to be hunted for in order that he be given the head dress, blanket and other artifacts that belonged to the camp but the chief was in charge of and guarded with his life.

Maude Elsie, Savannah, Nadine, Dixie, and the rest were happy to hear that Leo would be chief. Indeed when Leo came to the general store to buy the canned milk and the rolled oats for the old people in the camp, was very shy and took the honor with humility. He had to be coaxed into the kitchen where he was given a cup of coffee and the Indian sweet bread Savannah had learned to make from the camp. Leo swept the depot boarding house and the folks around the general store clean as far as friendship is concerned and asked if his wife may now trade at the general store, as she was not allowed until now. A cry went up throughout the ladies at the store. Maude Elsie assured him that all was well and they were surprised that his wife was not allowed in the store by the Indians.

Leo Two Feathers lineage could be traced to the Seminoles' greatest chief of all Chief Osceola. Since Chief Osceola's death in 1838 at Fort Moultry, near Charleston, South Carolina, his lineage was kept on going by his wife, who he married (a braves widow) in the first year of being chief, and now her young children aided by Coacoochee and his father King Phillip who had escaped from Fort Moultry a short time before Osceola's death. They slipped quietly into the cypress swamps along the Santee and Cooper rivers, then aided by the escaped slaves along the route through Savannah, and Brunswick, Georgia, across the St. Mary's river around Jacksonville and to the home of his wife and the land where his eldest son was a stranger. The band of family Osceola later led by Billy Bow Legs were led by Little Tiger to the edge of the large lake later given his name and after Little Tiger renamed himself at eighteen years of age Billy Bow Legs ran with Chief Chipco until he could stomach no more of Chipco's bad treatment of the whites in the Hillsborough (later Polk County) County. This camp pulled away from Chipco and later when Chief Chipco was camped on Bannon Island in Lake Hamilton, the Bow Legs camp were the source of the leak as to where Chipco had hidden himself, his band of around fifty braves, women and children.

Therefore Leo Two Feathers grew up to be a man of great character, honest and brave a good hunter provider and now he would be chief of this camp of Indians who would later become members of the Seminole Tribe. Chief Leo would be an emancipator of the Indian women in his camp and trading and buying would become the greatest cause to keep the women from the demeaning work that could be done without the abuse the women took in the game of the Indian life. Where items could be bought in jars or cans they were bought or traded for. The goods that the Indian women made, sewed, smoked, dried or picked such as herbs were used for trading or bartering for other goods.

A powerful bond was struck when the women of the scrub and the

Indians were camped nearby, as more and more of the scrub was giving way to open fields for farms and citrus groves and were beginning to dot the edges of the lakes with the ready source of abundant water for the young citrus trees and the gardens and farms.

The young Indian men who wanted to earn extra money for goods and even to buy land would work for the white man and became stable hands, and general house and grounds gardeners. The women of the camp would hire as waitresses and maids to some of the richest land owners and the large homes, especially in Bartow where there were lawyers, judges, county commissioners and the like for where there was an opportunity the young women and braves would take the job and work hard and well for their employers.

All the new way of the Indians were also taught by the women in the scrub. Maude Elsie, Mary Sykes-Remmick, Orange Blossom, Brittany Crocket, Savannah, Ford, Nadine and all the others would help the Indian girls on a one on one, as a mentor and not only for the labor which they surely got from the Indian women, but the training worked both ways, the whites' learned the Indian ways and the Indians learned the whites' ways. The Indian women learned to sew on the hand crank sewing machines, how to can foods and not poison anyone, how to bake, cook, and keep the homes clean, neat and safe.

The men learned forestry, farming, animal husbandry for the improvement of cattle, sheep, goats, swine, domesticated rabbits, the growing new use of fertilizer both natural and chemical. Cattle buying, selling, and breeding, breaking horses to ride and to harness. Building homes, barns and other buildings needed for the home or ranch. They learned to survey and measure. This made schooling type of education more important to the children and adults.

So as Leo Two Feathers led his camp into the new century the people followed him and enjoyed the highest standard of living of all the camps and tribes in Florida and started a wide spread issue of education throughout the entire peninsular of Florida. But the sad truth was that a lot of the braves with little or nothing to do started and ended their adult life with alcohol. The waste of the Seminole was a terrible waste of manhood and an entire generation.

WORSE THAN WILD FIRE

Young Billy entered the front door of his home and went directly to the divan and laid down. Blossom went to check on him as he hardly spoke to her when he entered the house. She saw that he was flushed and his ears were fire red, she felt his forehead and found him hot with fever. She told Billy to strip to his underwear and to go get into the tub they used for bathing. Blossom poured cold water over him until he was immersed in the cold water.

She went to the main house and asked for Mary Sykes to come and see what was wrong with Billy.

Mary went to the house with Blossom and found Billy was not conscious. They took him to his room and striped him of his clothes, dried him and put him in his bed. He started to have chills, they covered him with quilts. Mary asked Blossom to heat one of the quilts in the oven of the stove and put that over him next to his skin.

Blossom pulled the covers back from Billy and saw large splotches of a strange color of red. She placed the warm quilt over him and the other covers to keep the warmth in and told Mary about the spots on Billy's body.

Mary looked at Blossom and then at Billy, then said, "Do not leave the house and do not let Billy out of the bed, I think he has rheumatic fever and you must watch him that he gets enough to drink and that you let him "go" in the chamber pot that you will look for blood in his pee."

Mary rushed to the office and had Tom telegraph Claude at Tanners depot and general store for Doctor Zimmerman. The doctor was found at the depot having a piece of pie and a cup of coffee.

Claude told the doctor what had happened and what she had done to treat the boy and asked the doctor to come as soon as possible.

Dr. Zimmerman wrote some orders and slid them across the table to Claude and said, "Here, send this to Mary and tell her I am on my way to the Bent Penny Ranch. Tell her that no one, and I mean NO ONE! Is to go near that child and that Blossom is not to leave the house for any reason other than a house fire."

The doctor turned to Maude Elsie and asked, "Has little Billy been around here in the last two weeks?"

"Why, yes he came up the day that his grandfather died, he was looking for the old Indian. He has been around almost every one from here to the Bent Penny Ranch," Maude Elsie told the doctor.

"MAN!" The doctor almost shouted, "That's the worse news that I could hear, The Indian camp will be down with this illness in just a few days. Maude Elsie, where is that large tent that you all had a few years back? Is it still good enough to use as a quarantine hospital for the next month? Do you have any sulphur? If you do take a teaspoon full, put it into a tin can with enough alcohol to start it burning and let it burn in every room in the depot and the general store, that will include the music man's wagon too," the doctor ordered as he finished his coffee and pie.

The telegraph was clicking its message across the wire and would soon be listened to by everyone as they waited to either come down with the illness or finding out they were not going to would begin helping the women of the scrub nurse the sick ones back to good health.

By the end of the week fourteen people had come down with the illness and the supply of sulphur was getting low. The doctor sent two men to Kissimmee to the drug store there to buy more of the drug and said, "Get the sulphur even at gun point." and sent a note with the men to the pharmacist at the apothecary.

The women who did not get sick would nurse around the clock, or would be at the wash pot boiling clothes, bead sheets, quilts, and night clothes worn by the ill ones. The washing went on night and day, sweat would run down the women's face, arms, chest and back, as the choking smoke of the sulphur burning in the house and in the tent made their eyes water and gave them a cough. They began wearing bandanas over their mouth and nose. Even the Indian women in the camp picked herbs and roots, made tea and crushed the leaves to extract the oil from the camphor tree leaves, pine needles, oak bark and pine gum.

The coffee pot, pan cakes, soup, toasted bread and when time would permit a pie or two to give the working women a little something extra with their food. Bacon, eggs were cooked all day, as there was little time to cook a ham or roast a beef. But sweet potatoes and baked Irish potatoes were constantly being baked for those who could keep solid food down.

Four days into the epidemic the first Indian died and was taken out of the tent and buried in the ground. The dead man was an elderly brave who battled pneumonia for three days but could not fight any longer, then expired.

The women dealt with the death and would mourn him and several others after the sickness left.

Savannah was exhausted and as she started to enter the tent she collapsed almost in the doctors arms, he picked her up and put her to bed. As soon as she came around he gave her a drink that included secobarbital, she slept for twenty four hours to awaken with a hangover which the doctor cured with a cup of coffee and a good breakfast.

The doctor made everyone of the workers, from that time and for the duration, start sleeping after twelve hours on duty, that included him.

Soon the depot boarding house was empty of sick folks and was used for the care givers to sleep and rest. The food and coffee was continuos from the kitchen as Nadine, Dixie, Fawn and Maude Elsie cooked and cleaned in shifts too. A few of the men were washing pots and pans for the women and other women washed and scalded the dishes and silverware. They carried water and pumped water until they thought their back would break but there were folks needing their help and that thought would make them work a little harder and longer until their shift was over and they were glad they had to rest.

An extra washpot was brought in just to keep water boiling for the kitchen and the ladies doing the washing.

Although at the outset there were six or eight cords of wood cut and split the fires of the washpots, stoves and cook stove ate into the piles of wood until the alarm was sounded and eight men got saws and went to the woods for oak and pine trees. The mules pulled the sleds to the wood lot and other men unloaded the sled and started cutting the logs into lengths and the men who were splitting took over to finish the labor of making the firewood.

Night and day, and day after day the sickness stayed its course then, after fourty three days there were no new cases of the fever. The doctor was driving back and forth from the depot to the Bent Penny Ranch, treating the sick ones. For those who succumbed to the illness, he wrote their death certificates for all persons white and Indian alike.

As they healed, the people were hungry and thirsty, so the work now settled onto the kitchen and the cooks of the two entities and food was getting to the point that the stores at the Tanners general store were low and getting lower by the day, they had to make the trip to Kissimmee, Bartow, Lakeland, and Harris's corners, for any food stuffs they could find.

At first most of the towns nearby were afraid that the disease might spread to them and would not trade with Spurgeon until the doctor came and really gave the holdouts the tongue lashing that only he could get away with and everyone trusted good ole doc Zimmerman.

They were actually afraid that the doctor would give them the sickness and as a result of his furry delivered the food to the general store, then Spurgeon, Maude Elsie and Mary Remmick saw to it that the two places and the Indian camp were fed.

Billy, now well and healthy saw his mother and went to her and hugged her then kissed her on the cheek and said, "Thanks Mama, for all you did for me. Now wont you get some rest? You look like you could sleep for a week." There was little spring in his step as was true with all who got over the disease. They found that they had to walk slowly and rest often as their heart must regain the strength that the fever had so badly removed from the person.

The doctor opened an office at Tanners Depot and put Savannah Ford in charge and thus his practice was spread through the county with able bodied women he trained to be nurses and care givers to the sick and afflicted.

Few if any animals got the sickness or if they did they died and were buried or rotted in the field or scrub. A surprising number of birds had died throughout the county and most of them were consumed by wild animals which didn't seem to be bothered by the disease that had killed the birds, if it was the same organism.

As things slowly got back to normal and the horses and wagons transverse the Bent Penny Trace, there was a noticably drop in the numbers of cows that were kicked out of the scrub that year and as a result the thought came to the cowboys that they should let the cows alone this spring and see if nature will help the breed come back some and see if the numbers would come back.

Some of the cowboys had to get jobs around the county and a few hired on to the Western Union and the railroad as track men and linemen. Since poles had to be replaced and on the railroad the crossties had to be replaced and the trackage realigned.

The cowboys were not as adapted to the turn of the Gandy Dancers as were the black men that had to teach the white cowboys how to move the track with a forty-five pound bar and the tapping on the rail until the callers and the tune and the word was given and the men gave a loud "HUH" and the track would miraculously straighten and they would tap, tap, tap their way to the next crook in the rail where the song would start again the track would give to the effort and so it went through the spring and summer, when fall was upon the land the newly producing citrus groves were in the need of harvesting the oranges and grapefruit. The cowboys began to drift toward the groves for jobs and pay lower than they had become accustom. They simply did what was necessary to get along and make do with what they had. Some of the men had sold their horses and saddles to make sure that their family was fed.

Spurgeon Tanner and Maude Elsie had the income of the depot and the general store though the amount of business was way off from last year but every one was feeling that pinch. The growers did well with the cheap labor they had for picking the fruit and as the year drew to a close the people throughout the county and the scrub was feeling better about the new year coming up.

Most of the people were now healthy and those that wanted to work got through the summer and fall with a little to spare and not a lot to show for the year of hard work in the scrub. At jobs they were not accustom to and money that just made do.

RING IN RING OUT

The chime of the anvil accepting the blow of the hammer, seemed to make the wintery day at the Tanner's a little less bleak. The sky was a dark gray and there had been little if any sunshine in the sunshine state for several days. The warm feeling of the day came from the blacksmith working his magic on the iron which was heated and transformed into what ever was needed at the time. To see the sparks fly as the hammer made the anvil ring again and again until the misty swosh of the iron being doused in the waiting bucket of tempering water.

Maude Elsie, Savanah, Nadine and Dixie were all humming the same tune to the beat of the black smith's hammer, as they flitted about in the depot's lobby. Christmas was just a week away and a lot still had to be done as the women were working till late at night preparing for the winter feast on Christmas Day.

What spirit. What gaiety, as the boxes of ornaments were brought from the attic and the items placed around the room and the kitchen, they were waiting for the tree to be brought in as it was time to cut the tree and erect it in the lobby almost touching the ceiling.

Some what of a clamor arose from the dooryard as the screen door banged open and the huge tree was whisked into the lobby by five strong men and set up on its pedestal and in its place so the candles when lit could be seen through the long glass doors of the stagecoach depot, turned boarding house.

The men waited for an invitation for a cup of hot coffee but it was not forth coming, rather another order from Maude Elsie to get the bay berries which were red as holly but more fragrant. So out they went to the southeast bay head where the bay was thicker and they seemed more red too. When they had the bed of the wagon full they returned to the depot and started unloading the wagon, and this time they let sufficient cold air in the lobby that the thought of hot coffee crossed the ladies minds and naturally the men were invited to sit at the table and have the warming liquid with the ladies.

Bad idea.

The ladies thought up more things to do than they could get done in a week or two. So with the coffee finished the men went back out side to tackle the manly jobs they were wont to do. Wood needed chopping and sawing, stock needed water and the stalls needed to be mucked out.

Without the men under foot the women got back to the organizing the up coming holiday and the wonderful treats that were to come from the kitchen. The Yankee minced meat was in the crock stewing away under the influence of the alcoholic liquid that even yet came from the Doolie boys still, no one was sure who was running the still but as long as the product was used for medicinal purposes it seemed to be ok to administer a dram here or there.

Savannah and Nadine were in charge of the pies and cakes and with the wood pile still up and the flour, butter, eggs, sugar and milk still plentiful the sweet treats were rolling out of the ovens with a sound form of consistency.

The smoke house was billowing out smoke as turkeys, hams, ribs, bacon, beefs, ducks and quail were curing in the sweet smoke of the different wood that were being fed the fire and the wood burner was stoked night and day until Maude Elsie said, "that is enough, Spurgeon."

The telegraph key was kept busy from the Bent Penny Ranch as what they were going to add to the mix of holiday food and fun. The children were the hardest to handle as they knew that there would be a visit by Father Christmas, bringing toys and goodies with him on his visit. The boys and girls could hardly wait until the wonderful holiday, now just hours away.

Until late afternoon the smithy's anvil and hammer sang to the settlement that the women noticed they were sleepy. Their eyes burned and watered, causing them to yawn often then notice that the men were working slower than this morning. What is causing them to feel so sleepy, that smoke house and the wood smelled so good but they had to go and get the fire eater and their hoses, perhaps now they now have the new hoses voted on in the past to have in the event there was a fire in the church before services.

Claude thought of the little Frankin Sense Tree it was now in the ground making new roots and should be left alone, except for an occasional trim with the pruning shears.

A group of men on horse back and new to the area were nearing the settlement when a tiny lady stepped from the door way of the general store and smartly walked across the clay trace and into the scrub. The men were wont to have a little fun with the small lady and as they parted to move into the scrub to surround her they found a small campsite, as they started to move through the campsite. The lady appeared from behind a wagon with a twelve guage coach gun and both hammers cocked, "Now jist whot ere ye a messin 'bout ma camp fer?"

Now since she was surrounded they thought they would have the upper hand but three of her sons walked out of the scrub behind the men.

"Yeah, whut wuz it youens wont here?" the second voice asked.

"We don't want nuthin and if you bees a mind to weuns kin go now and finish our dealing wit Mr. Spurgeon, over yonder," the older man said as he started to wheel his horse around just to see who was behind him.

"Whut business you got with me?" Spurgeon asked.

"We got nigh on to five hundred head o' beefs back down the trail a mile er two," the older man answered again.

"I aint in tha cow buyin business, you need to talk to Mr. Coxin over to tha Bent Penny Ranch, they bees in tha cow buyin business. Now I know who you men are and I don't want you to even disturb the leaves in this here campsite, now git and I mean git!" Spurgeon spoke loudly and got the message across as the men turned their horses very carefully and started out of the scrub.

Spurgeon spoke to the family and said, "We been gonna have ouren Christmas dinner in the next day or two and on Christmas day we would be privileged to have youens over ta tha dinner." then Spurgeon turned and headed out of the scrub watching for the men he had just runoff.

They were across the trace and were tied up at the hitching rail on the side door of the general store, all seven of them.

"Uh oh, we got trouble," Spurgeon whispered to himself as he eased around to the back door of the general store and entered quietly.

He heard voices in the store and could not hear the telegraph clicking as it usually does. Spurgeon cracked the door open a little and peered inside the store with one eye.

One of the men had his back to the door and as he listened he could hear the fear in Savannah's voice. Maude Elsie had not spoken yet and that gave Spurgeon a clue that she was likely as not over in the depot.

"We wont y'all ta give usens some grub and sum of them pies in tha safe whut youens is got baked up," Spurgeon heard one of the men say and the men shifted as though they were going to move on Savannah. Spurgeon stepped through the door and said, "Hold it. I knowed youens wuz up ta with your sneakin round cheer."

Maude Elsie heard Spurgeon talking and went into the store from the depot with the other twelve guage shot gun and the men wilted when they had one in front and one behind them with guns. "Now tell you what you men shuck those guns and gun belts then you gonna march to the barn where you all will spend Christmas like the first Christmas family in a barn with the animals," Maude Elsie ordered.

The men walked out and down the four steps onto the white sugar sand of the Florida scrub, as they walked they noticed that several men appeared from different places to watch the procession. They saw the shotguns and Winchester as they neared the barn. Ski was the first to the barn door, he slid the latch bar back and swung the doors wide open. Two of Sturgeons men came in the barn and took the ropes and slung them across a rafter one rope for each of the men.

They were tied with their hands behind them with the rope over the rafter and then pulled to where their arms were almost shoulder high and they were tip toeing to keep the taut ropes from pulling out their shoulder sockets. They were talking to each other and threatening Spurgeon and the people there at the depot and general store. Soon they saw how futile that was and started at each other as they had to blame their predicament on someone other than themselves.

The telegraph was busy with the sheriff in Bartow and as he read the

story the telegrapher wrote, Sheriff Mel ordered the jail wagon to go and get the seven men from the Tanners place.

"You know that ole Spurgeon aint got much truck with people that don't treat his people right," the sheriff said as he buckled on his gun belt and reached for his hat.

"Dugger, you git them men and git back here I want them behind bars before Christmas, do you understand?"

"Yass suh," the old black man answered and went to the livery stable to get the jail wagon.

A quick rain shower came up and with a rush and high winds the rain wasn't enough to even settle the dust. But Dugger harnessed the horses and led them to the jail wagon and soon the heavy rig was rumbling down the Bent Penny Trace, and Dugger was singing a Negro spiritual over the rattle of the wagon.

As the rain was the lead of the cold front the closer the jail wagon got to the Tanners place the colder the tempature got in the scrub. The wind was blowing about ten miles per hour and began to cut right through the jacket Dugger had slipped on before he left the livery stable. Now he wished he could stop and build a fire just to warm up but he knew the sheriff Mel would probably skin him alive if he didn't get the prisoners back to Bartow before Christmas.

Dugger was shivering uncontrollably when he tied the hitch up to the rail in front of the general store. He climbed the steps and entered the store. There was no one in there so he looked through the arch way leading to the depot and saw the roaring fire in the lobby stove and he headed for the warmth of that stove.

"Look who the cats dun drug in . . ." Spurgeon said as Dugger walked into the lobby and almost embraced the large stove standing in the center of the depot lobby. Spurgeon and the other men were sitting around the stove, while the women were in the kitchen putting supper together.

"I don't know who it is just come in," Maude Elsie said. Then she continued, "it'll have a mouth to feed," and the women laughed at Maude Elsie as she took down the clean white dishes stacked in rows on the shelf over the bread box. She placed the dishes at each place and put three extra on the sideboard.

"Spurgeon, will you bring all the folks into the table and let's ask the

blessing before the diner gets cold?" Maude Elsie spoke loud enough over the drone of the men talking in the lobby.

"Hey Dugger you gonna eat supper with us tonight?" Spurgeon asked and got an immediate affirmative reply.

"Yass suh, I sho was a hoping fer some of miss Maude Elsie's vittles," Dugger replied with a grin from ear to ear.

Maude Elsie and Savannah served the meat and potatoes, Nadine served the green beans and the collard greens, Dixie and Fawn placed platters of warm bread on the long table. Nadine also had just finished the huckleberry cobbler and placed it out on the ironing porch to cool until the boarders and others were ready to eat the wonderful dessert.

After supper the team was unhitched and put into the feeding lot for their supper of oats, corn, hay and water.

The tempature was still dropping when Dugger finally hitched the team back up to the jail wagon and the men led the prisoners one by one to the waiting wagon. The men complained about it being too cold and asked for their bed rolls from their saddles. The bed rolls were tossed into the jail wagon without checking them for any weapon first. The men sat straight up in the wagon and real close together to help block the wind. It didn't help much.

The trip back to Bartow started with a jerk as the horses pulled the load as the large wagon jolted to a start behind the team of horses. "Hard drivin a four up with col' hans," Dugger said as he whipped the horses up and was glad that Spurgeon had lent him a nice warm over coat and scarf to wrap up his mouth and ears from the bitting cold.

Soon the lights of the Tanners general store was no longer visible and the only light was from the moon and stars reflecting off the clay trace as they headed back to Bartow.

Along about eleven o'clock the wagon eased to a stop as Dugger had drifted off to sleep and the team of horses lost the feel of the reins and stopped walking. The shouts of the men in the jail wagon woke him and he slapped the reins on the horses and cracked his whip. The jail wagon started rolling again, but the men kept fussing till Dugger said, "Whut youens is a hollarin 'bout? You know that iffen ya gotta pea you stick it through tha back bars an go, but iffen yore sick then you gotta stay in tha wagon till ah gits yall ta Bart-tow, now jist you hush!"

But the older man of the group kept yelling that there was something wrong back in the wagon. And to come check the wagon might be on fire or something. But Dugger had heard them all and since he didn't smell smoke he was sure that the wagon was not on fire, besides there wasn't anything on the wagon that would burn since it was made of solid iron plates and the only ventilation was from the single door with bars on it from top to bottom. So the wagon drove on toward Bartow as the night grew colder and the wind blew to make the cold even more bitting.

"We need to get warn," came the cry from the wagon and then as Dugger felt the wind even through the over coat the Spurgeon had loaned him his hands were numb and he needed to get his legs and feet moving too.

There was a large clearing up ahead where the wagon could pull over into the white sand and there was enough of an area that the wind wouldn't blow any embers into the forest and cause a forest fire.

Dugger pulled the wagon over into the scrub sand and got down from the seat high above the iron roof of the jail wagon. He walked around the wagon where the old man had a gun and he ordered Dugger to unlock the jail wagon door. As he unlocked the door one of the men kicked it open catching Dugger in the face and chest. He fell back onto the scrub sand and as he did a shot rang out from the door of the wagon and Dugger felt the bullet burn into his chest. He did not move again. The men took his gun and gun belt, the short barrel twelve guage from under the drivers seat and unhitched the horses. Three of them rode double as they took the wagon team as their rides to freedom and soon the four horses and seven men were again out of sight in the scrub. The escape was complete on the day before Christmas Eve.

A BLEAK CHRISTMAS EVE

The gray sky was the nell and toll of the day as the dark sky seemed to foretell the time that was rapidly trotting toward the Tanners Depot Boarding House and General Store. The gaiety of the family atmosphere rose to the crescendo of merriment and singing as the pump organ was being played and carol after carol sang out from the pipes within the oaken body of the instrument. So much so, in fact, that no one heard the four horses gallop up and being tied to the hitching rail. Not one soul heard the seven men as they mounted the steps to the front door of the depot.

As the escapees burst through the door with guns drawn the surprise was complete. Silence fell on the room and at first was deafening to all of the merry makers in the lobby of the depot.

The four men were surprised also as they realized that there was only one man in the whole place and he was sitting with his back to the wall listening to the telegraph as it click-clacked out Christmas greeting to anyone who was within ear shot of the receiver. Claude slipped the knife switch to the Bent Penny trunk and tapped a quick S. O. S. To cover the clicks Maude Elsie asked in a loud voice, "Wont yall come in out of the cold and wind? Have some punch and cookies. These girls have been baking these treats for a solid week now and they need to be et."

The seven men walked into the depot looking in all the doors to see where the men were, then they ordered Claude out of the Western Union office and told him to sit over by the women. The strangers started eating the cookies. One of them went to the kitchen to get the coffee pot. The coffee was on the back of the stove where it would stay hot but not boil and get bitter. He brought the coffee back into the lobby of the depot then sent Savannah to get the cups for them. They drank the coffee black and ate three of the pies that were in the pie safe beside the stove in the kitchen.

One of the men decided that he wanted a drink of whisky and started yelling at Maude Elsie, "Old woman, you got any whisky in here?"

"This isn't a bar or a saloon sir and there is no whisky in this house." Maude Elsie spoke loud and direct to the man. Just as she finished saying that she noticed the outside door to the wood box silently close. She thought about that and soon her curiosity was satisfied as she saw the cat walk through the kitchen. The cat or any animal for that matter was not allowed in her house. She knew that the cat was as wild as a haint and could not be picked up by anyone. This one came to the kitchen door then hissed and turned back. Soon two more cats were in the house and Maude Elsie knew that Spurgeon was doing it to let her know how many men he had on the outside of the house and if any of the men started anything they would be inside faster than the men could get to their guns. That's what she hoped anyway.

Savannah and Nadine saw the cats too and wondered but said nothing and when Cloud and Fawn saw they almost asked the question, "What are the cats doing in the house?" but as they watched Maude Elsie and Savannah they both realized they were going to be used for something later against the bad men.

The men decided that Nadine and Savannah would have to move up stairs and please them, or so they were ordered. Savannah invited two of them to her room and bade them follow her up the stairs to her room. They walked up the stairs and Nadine followed with a man in tow also.

When they reached the room there were two of Spurgeon's men in each room and as the men followed the girls into the room they were rendered unconscious with the barrel of a rifle and they were caught as they fell and thrown over on the bed. That left four men down stairs and in a while Savannah went down and told the older man that the two were sleeping.

"Why you stupid woman why didn't you try to climb out a window and escape?" the old man asked.

"You must be kidding, it must be a twenty foot drop outside my window, I am not as stupid as you think I am. Beside I thought the young boy might want to come with me and return to you as a man." Savannah touted as she took the youngest boy by his shirt sleeve, "You may need a bath first, though."

The young boy jerked away from Savannah and said, "I aint a takin no bath in this here weather, a body might catch the . . . the . . . p-monia er sumpin. I aint a going wit cha."

The older men laughed at the young boy and then one other volunteered to go with Savannah, by which befell the same treatment, rifle barrel and all. That left three, and one of them was a snot nosed boy of eighteen, and perhaps not so long at that age if truth was known.

Maude Elsie offered the older man another pie and when he reached for it she dropped it on his foot, as she started to bend over to reach the pie she quickly drew his side arm which was a Colt 44-40, and as she did she cocked the pistol and fired it in to his chest. The man dropped like a slippery rock and lay dead on the floor. The Colt was cocked again and the second man fell to his death on her Depot lobby floor. The young kid couldn't get his gun out of the holster, whether too shocked or nervous, the other three women grabbed him and made him lie on the floor under the threat of the third shot coming from his dead daddy's pistol.

Spurgeon, Ski Shalen, Jake Owen, and Norm Tracy came from every possible ingress to the room and kitchen including the wood box beside the stove.

The four men who were rendered useless to the group were taken to the barn and tied to the rafters as before but this time the rope was around the neck and they were standing on a round log from the fire wood pile outside the barn. If they were to slip off the log they would be hanging around in the barn the next morning.

Claude wasted no time getting in touch with Sheriff Mel and telling him what had taken place there and where the other's were, that two were dead from gunshot wound, one by his own gun, the other four who were hanging in the barn were captured by means that should not be said on the telegraph wire.

Sheriff Mel came in to the lobby about six hours after the incident. He told the people that he had found Dugger and the jail wagon and this time there would be no bed rolls in the wagon for the men's comfort, as the duffel had been used to wrap Dugger's body in.

The four horses had been put in the barn and fed while they were waiting for the sheriff to get there. After he arrived the horses were harnessed again and led back to the wagon. The five men were ordered to place Dugger's body in to the jail wagon and to respect the dead as they would have a special treat when the Judge finds that they killed Deputy Sheriff Dugger.

As Christmas morning dawned the jail wagon was driven out of the yard and on toward Bartow and the county jail. The men arrived with several different malady's one of which was frostbite of the fingers and toes. Strange marking showed up on their bodies but no one could say what had happened to the five men, but what difference does it make they are going to hang the day after Christmas.

The air was once again gay as the folks at the Tanners Depot and General Store began celebrating Christmas with the pump organ playing so many Christmas tunes and all the festivities began again and this time was a charm as everyone chipped in to make this the merriest of Christmases. There was enough food, there were enough pies, cakes and cookies.

Presents and gifts were exchanged and the nicesest was a wedding ring for Nadine from Claude.

The conversation was polite and there was no mention of the intrusion of the seven men on that morning, as the whole table was loaded with food and the people there were enjoying the food now. As the hard work of the past days and weeks slipped from their memories the women of the scrub enjoyed the feast and the day off from the normal activities and pressures of the day and the times as they ate, drank and enjoyed the wonderful Christmas feast.

The organ was again playing the tunes of the Christmas season, but now a quartet of singers were gathered around the instrument and the organist, the singers were in tune as others not so talented sat around the lobby singing with the rest of the group.

Spurgeon and Ski slipped from the room and sauntered out to the stable to check on the livestock, as they had to be fed and watered. There was little or no conversation between the two men as they went about their chores in the barn and stable. Ski climbed the ladder to the hay loft and pitched down a rick of hay which Spurgeon forked into the stalls occupied by the horses, mules, cows and goats. The animals began munching on the hay and when the combination of oats and corn were poured into the feed buckets the hay was abandoned until later in the evening when they would again start munching on the golden straw.

Soon Jake Owen came into the barn with Little Cloud at his heels, the child had picked Jake as somewhat of a figure that needed to be watched and copied as best she could. At four years old she would not wear a dress she had to have her blue jeans and boots with a shirt of white or of light color just like Jake would wear daily.

"Unca Jake, does them cow and horse critters know that it is Christmas?" Little Cloud asked in her "I am very interested and I really want to know voice" which was a little deeper than her normal voice as she tried to mimic every thing that Jake did when she was around him.

At first it was an annoyance to Jake, having the little person tagging along and when he would climb a board or split rail fence Little Cloud scampered up the fence too. There were questions, answers and whys interminably. That kid wanted to know everything until Jake felt like a school teacher and a surrogate father to the little beauty.

Yes, she was a beautiful child and the Christmas season was especially wonderful as she was so sure that Jake was really Father Christmas, and spared no notion in telling him so. Her hair was coal black and her eyes were too with dark eye brows and lashes, her eyes seemed to look all the way through him. Her skin was olive and smooth. She would comb her hair and as soon as she was dressed would put her little Stetson style hat over her locks and she was ready for the day.

Christmas morning and day suited the children well as they were surprised at the gifts they received and the stockings were gorged with fruit, candy and small gifts. They all were happy to see the dinner start as by noon or there about they were tired and hungry from all the activities with their new toys.

Little Cloud picked up the lid of the feed bin and let out a squeal and slammed the lid back down. The men in the barn thought she had her hand caught in the lid but when they saw her back away from the bin they knew there was something else wrong in that large box.

"Rat, rat . . . in the feed bin," she shouted as she ran for the barn door which was closed against the cold wind outside. She could not quite reach the door latch and stood there with her back to the door whimpering. That was the first time any of the men knew of that Little Cloud was afraid of anything that moved, including snakes, but she was defiantly afraid of rats.

Jake got an axe handle and Ski through the feed bin lid open, as the rat jumped he batted the rat alway across the barn and it hit the barn door just to the right of where Little Cloud was standing.

Another scream and this time some words came from Little Cloud that made the men in the barn blush. Where did she get those words? Each man looked at Jake with questions in their eyes, but Jake looked just as surprised.

It was Little Clouds self imposed duty to feed old nanny the goat and her kids. Now that the rat had been dispatched she calmly went back to the feed bin and dipped out two quarts of the oats and corn feed mixture, took it to the goat stall and unlatched the gate, as she went in the kids started muzzling into the feed can before she could pour the feed into the feed bucket almost knocking it out of her hands. She quickly poured the feed into the trough to get the greedy little goats out of the feed bucket.

Nanny was slow getting up and when she did stand up Little Cloud let out another squeal. This time out of love. "Come, look, unca Jake, muster Ski, muster Smurgeon, come look at the new baby goats that nanny found last night, what a wonderful Christmas present we have now with the new baby goats," Little Cloud shouted to the top of her tiny voice.

When the feeding and bedding was complete the barn doors were again unlocked and the four came out and walked to the house, the nearer they got to the house the faster Little Cloud ran until she ran into the lobby shouting, "We gots new baby goats and I am so proud of old nanny. I think that is the best Christmas I could have, I think."

The adults laughed and the other children wanted to go see the babies right away but Maude Elsie nixed that plan as she announced that supper was ready and away the children went to eat the Christmas dinner again for supper this time.

While they were eating Little Cloud was entertaining them with her version of the rat episode and the greatest of all adventure was to find the new baby goats.

"Do the animals know that it is Christmas?" Little Cloud asked.

"Yes. And if you will be quiet for a little while I will tell you the story of the cattle at the midnight hour on Christmas morning," Maude Elsie told Little Cloud who hushed at once and looked at Maude Elsie with expectation, and silence.

"Every year at midnight the cattle where ever they are will stand up and turn toward the east then turn around and lie down again," Maude Elsie told the story in a short fashion so the children could ask questions. But they only looked at her like deer that had been spotted by lantern light. "They just do that and no body knows why," she continued.

"Do the animals . . . I mean the cattle know that it is Christmas?" one of them asked.

"It would seem so," Maude Elsie answered.

"Do goats know that it is Chwismus, aunt Maw Essie?" Little Cloud asked.

"Why sure they do, look what happened this Christmas," Maude Elsie answered.

Everyone fell into silence and there was a low pitch of some people speaking in low voices, there was the clink of the forks on the plates and spoons against the dishes as they dipped dressing, squash, green beans, turkey, ham from the smoke house, fresh bread, biscuits, gravy, home made pickles, jam and wild honey. For dessert there were pecan pies, apple pies, huckleberry pies and buttermilk pies, there were cakes, vanilla, chocolate, coconut and angle food cake served with preserved strawberries. Everyone finished eating and went back into the lobby to let it settle while Maude Elsie, Savannah and Fawn cleaned up the dishes and the left over food.

Claude went to the wood pile to bring in an arm load of fire wood for the cook stove to heat the water to wash the dishes. He picked up two logs and felt someone touch him on the back as he turned around there stood Nadine with the ring on her finger and as Claude dropped the wood she fell into his arms and would not leave until their personal passions were almost beyond the point of no return.

Claude took her arms from around his neck and eased her away saying, "We will have a time to our selves when we are married and we will enjoy each other the way we wish to tonight."

He picked up the fire wood and opened the wood box door beside the stove and placed the wood in the box until there was no more room in the box. When he walked into the kitchen he had another arm load of wood which he carefully stacked into the wood box and walked through the lobby into the Western Union Office, to listen to the conversation of the telegraphers and to think of what had happened at the wood pile and how much he loved Nadine and she loved him too. The triplets would never know any other father than him and he was surely going to be the best father these children will ever have. He then threw the switch over to the main Western Union Line and sent, "MERRY CHRISTMAS, YOU BET !" then signed off for the night.

YEAR AFTER YEAR

Spring time has come and in central Florida that means the heat is back. Regardless the time to plant the garden is here and with the moon being right with the "Almanac" the manure from the winters mucking the stalls is being hauled to the garden. The garden is a four acre plot just west of the general store where Spurgeon had cleared the woods and scrub of trees and stumps well enough that they could plant a spring garden and harvest the garden before time to plant the summer garden.

The spring garden will include cabbage, tomatoes, new potatoes, okra, beans, corn, gourds, cucumbers, and water melons. At the last minute four rows of peanuts were added.

The seeds were in the ground and with the mist from the barn stalls it would be a few days before the plants would stick their heads above the imbedded straw. With the Spring rains the garden will grow and yield prolifically by the last of May, and then while the men are plowing up the Spring garden to ready the field for the summer garden the women of the scrub will be canning the bounty from the early garden.

To see the plants grow, Maude Elsie walked again and again on daily trips to the garden to watch for new growth. The amazement of the wonderful garden always turns her thoughts to God and as she looks out across the four acres, she see's the corn already waist high and the beans ready to sprout, the tomatoes clinging to the wires along their rows, with all this wondrous beauty she thanks Him for the blessing and the beauty of the garden.

April turns to May and the garden is an array of good things to eat. The cabbages are really larger than a man's head, the tomatoes are in a different degree of ripeness, some green for use in making green tomato pickles and fried green tomatoes, the beans have already been picked over once the week before, now ready for picking again. The corn and the roasting ears are sweet and yellow as the morning sun, the gourds are hanging from the vines waiting to be picked and dried to make them into useful tools, such as dippers for the water buckets, dippers for the wash house, and bird houses for the purple martins which come and eat mosquitos every Spring.

The canning has begun and the glass jars are in the boiling wash pot being readied for the women to put up the peas, beans, tomatoes, corn, and cucumber pickles, both sweet and sour. The cabbages as they are ready are sliced on the mandolin and put into the stone crocks with salt and juniper berries to make sour kraut.

These new efforts of the women are done after the normal chores of washing, ironing, cooking three meals a day, tending the garden, making beds, baking bread, and milking the cows and the goat. There is little time for these women to have any off time of their own so they must go on doing their chores and getting some of them done long after dark and then there are the supper dishes to wash, dry and put away. There are then children to bathe or get ready for school the next day. There is so little time for the ladies to make up their faces or get dressed up for an ocaision, a barn dance or a social at the church, they enjoy these things but have to stretch to make the time for them.

Time was when the garden needed water it had to be toted from the stream not so near by. This chore was halted only long enough so that the women could go to the house and cook dinner or supper for the men. Some times the men were in the woods hunting for meat or for cattle or horses and would not be in until near supper time, so the women would work carrying water from the creek to slake the young plants thirst. Then after supper they would carry more water until each plant in the garden had been watered.

That was a hard time and as the years went by and things got better Spurgeon drove a well into the middle of the four acres and it didn't take so long to water the young sprouts as when the women had to tote the water from the creek. The well water was clean and cool and when one was thirsty it was like a drink from heaven. The women understood why the small plants enjoyed the well water so. Now and again Maude Elsie would get a thirst for the water from the garden pump, and would wander down into the garden, prime the pump and drink her fill of the cool liquid that God had furnished for them.

So now the days are just as long and the work is just as hard, the women are just as tired, and perhaps a little more so since the years are slipping behind one or two of them. Yet the relentless Florida heat, drought, storms, lightning, pestilence, and worry all build and are relieved when the crops start coming in to the house and kitchen.

Maude Elsie, Savannah, Dixie, Nadine, Fawn, Eunice Dunbar, Gladys Selmon and Birdy Ort all work and live at the Depot boarding house or near by along the Bent Penny Trace and all pitch in to get the work done and the now with the garden they are pressed into service as "sha-o cwoppers" as Little Cloud calls them, "Because they get a sha-o of the cwops form Aunt Maw Essie darden." Each of the women get to keep enough of the canned up vegetables, meat, tomatoes, pickles, and jams and jellies made from the guava trees dotted about the scrub and near the garden. The ladies get enough to last through the winter and can have more if they need for all they have to do is ask Maude Elsie. Plus there are alway jars and jars of food and fruit given to relative who visit the Boarding house and General store. Some of the product is sold in the store too.

Harold Richards had been the wood cutter and splitter. He kept the pots boiling for the laundry and the canning retort for boiling the cans and jars after they had been sealed with the product inside. Harold would use the devil sticks to probe the depths of the boiling water and remove every can and jar from the boiling pot when the time for them to be in the boiling water was finished.

Devil sticks, were two long flat boards about one inch wide, one half inch thick and about two or three feet long, they were glued, nailed or bound with thin rope or sinew onto an angular piece of wood about eight to ten inches long and as above attached to one end of the sticks forming a large pair of wooden tweezers. Since they were in and out of the boiling water they were called *devil sticks.*

There were few written receipts which were followed by the women as they canned the vegetables from the garden, they seemed to know what to add next to the mix, a pinch of salt, a cup of sugar, a shake of spices or what ever was called for. The finished products were always delicious, filling and healthy for the most part in early Florida pioneer canning and cooking.

Hot peppers were grown on the edges of the garden and as usual some child has to get the fiery fruit in the mouth as the pods are tantalizingly pretty with the red ripe and green pods. This time it was Little Cloud who sampled a pod of red pepper and was standing near the bush gaging and unable to breathe, she could not cry out to her mother or anyone else there in the garden. Savannah heard her gagging reflex and ran to her with a potato and she smashed the potato on a stump and took up the white inside of the tuber and forced it into the child's mouth. She picked the girl up and started to squeeze her in a hard hug until she was breathing again. At that time she sounded the alarm to her mother. Little Cloud gave the red peppers a wide birth from that time on and would warn everyone who came to visit the garden, "Don eet tha red pepp-o's, it huts u mouf."

That crisis behind them the planting, watering, picking and canning would go on as the women took to task each new plant that was willing to give up its bounty and make the finest of suppers sometime later.

The cabbages were showing too rapid of growth and were being picked so the families could have boiled cabbage, cabbage soup and stuffed cabbage. The hogs in the pen made short work of the tough outer leaves from the head and expected even more from who ever was near the pen.

Spurgeon was especially fond of boiled cabbage and potatoes with short ribs and rice with onions. The two dishes were placed on the table as often as the fresh cabbages were available then they made the sour kraut from the balance of the crop of cabbages.

The Fourth of July meant the work would be done and the day celebrated with a picnic, singing, fiddle and guitar playing, storytelling, and in the evening homemade fireworks. The children played and played in the dooryard and kept harassing the catch dogs which were watching the festivities from under the front porch. When a child would come too close the dog would get up and move further under the depot.

For this occurrence the calliope was hauled out of the barn, a fire stoked in the small boiler and played, but considerably quieter than the professor had played the instrument.

"Yankee Doodle", Dixie, Marching through Georgia and other

patriotic songs were bellowed forth through the scrub on that day of celebration.

Now that Summer was officially upon the habitants of the scrub were again back to work the very next day as the chores were forever on going and only the very small children had any time for playing and games. The long days and hard word was again in front of the women and the men who lived and toiled here in the central Florida scrub.

GROWING LIKE WEEDS

Old man Thurst's mule and wagon rumbbled up to the front of the general store. He got down and stepped up the steps and entered the store.

"Mawnin' miz Tanner," he said to Maude Elsie.

"Good morning, Edward," Maude Elsie replied.

"I got a hankerin fer sum sto bot vittles, 'n since ah gots ta pick up sum hay in tha wagon ah thot ah mount as well buy me some vittles too," Ed Thurst continued to Maude Elsie.

"What would you like, Edward?" Maude Elsie asked.

"Yall gots any peaches in a can?" Thrust asked.

"Yes, we do how many cans do you want?" Maude Elsie asked.

"Yess'um, ah wonts this here many," and Edward held up three fingers.

"Do you want Ski to load your wagon with hay, and do you want loose or baled hay?" Maude Elsie asked.

"Yes'um, ah needs nine bales o' hay," Ed replied.

"Do you want Harold to drive your wagon across the way and get the hay loaded? By the way if you will take the tenth bale you get it for free if you buy nine," Maude Elsie quoted Ed, and went to the door to call Ski or Harold in to move the wagon and load it with bales of hay.

Nadine had placed the triplets in a large wooden crate while she was doing her chores, Maude Elsie could watch the children, or Harold, who ever was in the store at the time.

Ed Thurst spied the children in the crate and stepped over beside them to talk to the three babies. All three were sitting now as almost a year had gone by since their birth. Ed poked at the children and with his motley looks and long beard the children at first were frightened of the man. Then with continued poking and making strange noises with his mouth the trio started giggling and cooing at the attention.

"You have a way with babies Mr. Thurst." Maude Elsie exclaimed as she reached up to the tins of peaches on the shelf.

"Well, yessum ah guess since ah wuz not higher'n a tater eye," Thurst said.

"Not much high . . ." Maude Elsie repeated under her breath as she put the tins of peaches on the counter. "I have heard a lot of comparisons in my day but I have never heard anyone say that before," and Maude Elsie smiled as she thought the realism over in her mind and could see a very young Edward Thurst standing next to a potato and not reaching the first eye of the potato.

"Mizz Maw Elsie, is youens seed a purty Tackie hoss these here bouts?" Edward asked Maude Elsie.

"What did it look like?" Maude Elsie asked.

"Hit wuz purty and almost strawberry roan hit shore iza purty little hoss, bout thirteen hands and has one white foot on to tha lef front. Hits aready broke to saddle and bridle, she done bees sa purty ah kin just bout cry anyhow," Edward said with his voice quivering.

Maude Elsie thought she might ought to move onto another subject, but when she did Edward would drag her back to the Marsh Tackie horse, so she went to the door, stepped out side picked up the piece of steel and hit the large dinner triangle just one lick. The tone went into the ears of the men in the barn now loading the hay wagon which was driven in by Edward Thurst.

Ski and Harold came inside the store and looked for some type of mess that customers sometimes made when they drop something and it breaks on the floor of the store.

"Relax boys," Maude Elsie said then continued, "Mister Edward Thurst has lost his new Marsh Tackie and would like to have her back. Do you all know of a loose pony?

"No maam," they said and started to turn to go to the barn to continue to load the hay wagon.

"Hold on now boys, this man needs to know where his horse is,"

Maude Elsie and the question hung in the air like a sheer curtain blown by a breeze.

"Well," Maude Elsie asked sternly and waited.

"I don't know maam, but Billy and the new chief was by here a day or two ago and they had a remuda of about ten horses coulda been they's was them," Harold answered.

"Where did they go with them?" Maude Elsie asked.

"Well, maam I don't rightly know they jist come from out'en tha scrub and across the trace, by the barn and back into the scrub. Why don cha have Claude telly-graph to tha Bent Penny Ranch to see if Billy knows where they were going, anyway that is what I'd do," Harold suggested.

"Good idea, Harold, now go back and finish loading the hay, then whip up your ride to the Bent Penny and find out from Billy where they went with the horses," Maude Elsie stated.

"Mr. Thurst, will you detail your horse to Harold here and let us try and locate your horse." Maude Elsie asked Edward.

"Yess'um, cept haint at aire telly-graph faster'n airy hoss? Kaint choo telly-graph tha Bent Penny quicker'n a man on a hoss kin ride to thar? Edward asked.

"Sure," Maude Elsie replied, then she walked into the Western Union office and asked Claud if he would wire the Bent Penny and see where the men had gone with the horses.

Claude sent the wire and waited for an answer. About fifteen minutes later the wire came back saying, "Billy and the Chief were heading for Kissimmee to the auction and would be about Fort Cummins about this time."

Claude wired Ft. Cummins, to inquire if the Chief and Billy had arrived with the horses.

The wire confirmed that they were indeed at the cow pens and holding the horses in a coral if someone wanted to inspect the horses. When they were informed of the identification of the horse like one of them had a white left front foot and blaze on the forehead.

"At cud been her, yessir at cud been my Tackie," Edward said and in a rush he asked, "Miz Maw Essie, kin ah bargin a riden hoss frum ya? Ah kin make hit ta fote Cummin afore dark an look see iffen at aires mah Tackie n ah'll be a cummin back ta mawnin.

"Let me call Spurgeon, I'll ask him," Maude Elsie told Mr. Edwards.

Harold went to the barn to get Spurgeon and when he got to the barn he found that Spurgeon was back in the garden plot and had to run another few yards to see if he could come to the office, Maude Elsie and Mr. Thurst needed him.

Spurgeon stepped inside the store and stood at the front door so as not to track the damp garden soil onto the store's floor.

"What do you all want?" Spurgeon asked.

"Do we have a horse we can let Mr. Thurst ride to Ft. Cummins on and return in the morning?" Maude Elsie asked her husband.

"Yeah, we's gots them music horsed an one o'them ort ta git him ta Fote Cummins 'n back ta here ta mawnin, they's broke ta saddle," Spurgeon rattled then headed back out the door.

"Before you go, Spurgeon, will you move Mr. Thurst's hay wagon around beside the barn and stable his mule until he gets back from Ft. Cummins," Maude Elsie asked as Spurgeon continued down the steps to the dooryard and crawled up on to the wagon seat and whistled the mule up. She pulled the loaded wagon around the barn and up the other side where Spurgeon unhooked the wagon and led the mule into the stall nearest the door. He wiped her down with a gunny sack gave her a bucket of oats and corn mixture, pitched her some hay and walked out of the barn. Just as he cleared the door the mule whinnyed at him and began eating the fine banquet set before her this evening.

Ski, had saddled the music horse and led him to the hitching rail to wait for Edward Thurst to climb astraddle and leave for Ft. Cummins.

Claude shouted to Edward, "Hey Edward, they have your Marsh Tackie and the deputy sheriff is holding Billy and Leo Two Feathers, for horse stealing. They are being taken to the lock up in Ft. Cummins right now. You need to tell them that they did not steal your horse but he got out and wandered to where they found her as a stray."

"Yeah, you send that rat cheer an now, that they aint not hoss stealers neither," Edward Thurst shouted back as he stepped up in the stirrup and spurred the big music horse away toward Ft. Cummins.

Ski and Harold brought in twelve or fourteen swamp cabbages and had that many more to strip to the bud which was the edible part of the swamp cabbage palm. The Sable palm as they are called in the north and down in the wilds of Florida they are called swamp cabbage. The Seminoles taught the whites to prepare and eat the delicacy of the swamp. Then it is up to the cook to prepare the swamp cabbage the way they were taught.

The Indians would fry fat salt pork till it was crisp usually about a quarter pound, after the meat was crisp the water about one gallon was added with pepper either red or black, but the red pepper used less or the meal would be too spicy to eat. While the water was coming to a boil they would peel the leaves from the bud of the palm tree until they came to the tender white part that was used as the swamp cabbage. The bud would be cut in about one inch pieces and the rings would be put into the boiling pot along with a cup of sugar where it was available. If they had wild onions they would slice six or eight onions and put them in the pot to cook with the swamp cabbages. The pot would be allowed to boil for as long as three to four hours, and as needed, water was added, but not very much at the time.

When the swamp cabbage was cooked they would all sit around the pot and eat the soup and eat the cabbages.

The Pioneer women made a variation of the Indian style swamp cabbage, they would fry the bacon and add several slices of smoked bacon, as the fat was rendered the yellow onions were peeled, chopped and added to the fat in the pot. When the onions were beginning to become opaque then the whole peeled tomatoes were added about six to eight depending on how many people she had to feed, about a gallon of water was added and when the stew was boiling hard the rings of swamp cabbage were added to the pot. Then salt and black pepper to taste and a cup to a cup and a half sugar was added to taste. The boiling continued for one hour when the coals were raked back and the pot allowed to stop boiling on its own. When the boiling was done the swamp cabbage stew was dipped out of the wash pot and put on the dinner table usually in several bowls or soup tureens. The meat served with the stew could be any type of wild meat or beef, pork, lamb, turkey, chicken, or some fried fish. Usually she cooked cornbread and biscuits. The newest rage at this time was sweet iced tea, and they even squeezed rough lemon or orange juice into the tea, depending on the individual's taste.

Maude Elsie took down her recipe book and placed it before her on the cutting board side of the drain board. The swamp cabbage was boiling in the washpot out by the wash house and the smoke house door was open and a large shoulder was being brought out.

Spurgeon dropped the smoked meat on the other side of the drain board and asked Maude Elsie, "You wont tha skin on tha ham er you wont me ta skin 'er, and put 'er in tha roas'in pan fer ye?"

"You can just make diamond cuts in the skin and I will do the rest and oh yes please do put it into the roasting pan for me." Maude Elsie answered even while she was reading the cook book and the women in the scrub called a recipe book. Most of them had only one word written on the extra white pages they put in books such as, Honeycake, Pineapple, for pineapple upside-down cakes, bananas or nanners for banana pudding. The trigger words would bring the recipe back to her mind instantly.

This time it was an angle food cake that Maude Elsie was fretting over since Mr. Thurst had mentioned the cake he likes is angle food cake, Maude Elsie thought, "I will try to make one of these cakes for the first time in my life."

The eggs, milk and flour were all there but what is cream of tartar she had never heard of that before. So she went to the Watkins Products catalog and sure enough there the stuff was and the Watkins man was due any day now so she would just wait on the angle food cake and for today she would bake a chocolate cake for the dessert tonight. But when she mentioned it to Nadine she said, "Let me bake the cake and you do your magic on the corn bread and biscuits, while the ham is cooking."

The ham was fully cooked from the smoke and heat of the smoke house so all it needed was to be warmed through and through.

Soon Little Cloud had Fawn and the Triplets all in the big wooden box with a cotton lining for the babies to play in. Harold called it the play corral and kept the bottom cushion soft with the duck feathers from the last falls duck hunt.

There was no special day but a feast was coming out of the kitchen of Maude Elsie, Tanner, with the help of Nadine, Savannah, Little Cloud, Dixie Dicksey, Birdy Ort, Gladys Selmon, and Eunie Dunbar. No one was given a task the task took them on. For instance Dixie and Gladys were on the back porch cleaning the collard greens, corn on the cob, and the potatoes both Irish and sweet. Nadine and Birdy were mixing the cake and Savannah was out by the washpot full of swamp cabbage stew, stirring the stew with the punch stick used when they washing, was being boiled in the same pot.

Three of the men Harold, Ski, and Jake were keeping the fire going by the washpot for Savannah. About every fifteen minutes Savannah would hand the punch stick to one of the men tending the fire and go into the kitchen to see what gossip she was missing and to cool off from the wash pot fire. The women laughed and joked about the weather, the men, the Indians, and the silliness of all this they were talking and giggling about.

The rooms in the Depot Boarding House were all full and two men were sleeping together in one room and even the mud room was being rented as a summer room, so when the dinner bell is rung they literally seem to pour out of every door in the house on their dash for the dinner table.

Maude Elsie and the other women served three meals a day at the Boarding house except on Sunday when there were no meals served there. There was bread, cheese, butter, jelly, honey, and left over cake, pie or what ever from the evening before.

Presently, Harold with an arm load of fire wood walked into the kitchen and was jeered out of the women's domain and made to feel that he had been the brunt of a joke of some sort from the women in the scrub.

At six p m on the dot the table was groaning under the weight of all the food which was on there and sagging toward the middle. Maude Elsie rang the dinner bell and the stampeding herd came rushing toward the dinner table and the side tables which were assigned to certain guests of the Depot Boarding House.

All of the women were kept busy refilling bowls and platters of meat, plates of biscuits, and cornbread. The women wondered where these people were putting all this food, but no one had a haver sack where any of the food was going, except in the stomachs of the people who were enjoying the meal and the conversation. Each person would speak to the person on either side of them and even when the meal was over the conversation then carried to the outside steps, swing, and railings.

"Must be a full moon tonight," Dixie commented as she carried plates from the dinner table to the kitchen to be washed, dried and put away. The pots were scrubbed and taken out side to be scoured with the white sand of the back dooryard.

The next day would be the day the women made the lye soap for the new year as Maude Elsie told Savannah the she hoped the good nature conversation would continue through tomorrow too.

The dishes done, washed dried and put away, the pots scrubbed and washed dried and put up, the kitchen stove cleaned with the black polish put on it and it is beginning to cool down. The women went to the front porch and sat with the men as some of the others had already turned in for the night.

The cool breeze blowing helped cool the women who had put in a long four hours to see that the meal was put on the table proper, and enjoyed properly too. The cool breeze even smelled of rain and it would help to get the wash pot clean for the next days use. The number one important tool in the pioneer womans life here in the scrub that versatile wash pot which was kept a handy distance from the back door of the house, the wash shed and the butchering bench, where the fat could be rendered and then kept in large tins to be used throughout the year for cooking, baking, and even for long time rust control on the families shot gun, pistol and rifle.

Now the rains are coming down and the wash pot is filling up, it will be ready for the next use when needed.

One by one the women, realizing that they are tired and sleepy, drift off to their own beds to sleep and dream of some one else doing the work while they watch and rest, Maude Elsie is the last to go to her bed as the lamps had to be turned down or blown out to dim the lobby and the halls so the people could sleep. As she eases into the bed beside Spurgeon he snorts and then continues with his snoring. Maude Elsie pats him on the hand and whispers, "Good night my love."

WEDDING BELLS IN THE SCRUB

Claude, had since Christmas given a ring to Nadine and she had said, yes, to all of the usual questions that go along with an engagement. She was hardly a blushing bride as she had been married before anyone knew her and sheriff Mel had decided to hang her for bank robbery, which the judge threw out when he found out the prisoner was pregnant. So Nadine wound up at the depot boarding house as an overnight guest and stayed as long as her ability to work for the room and board as well as the goat's milk for the triplets, now a year old and walking. The large wooden crate is still holding them but the next thing will be to climb over the walls of Jericho, as Claude calls the crate which is the life saver of both Nadine and the children, Joshua, Jacob and Sarah.

Claude has been the only father the triplets have known and now they even call him Da-da, which he loves and will beam like a search light when they call him da-da.

Then we have Harold Richards and Fawn, she has a baby, Little Cloud, and Harold no longer has to worry about the Indian cutting his throat anymore and he and Fawn are planning on marrying the same day as Claude and Nadine. Now none, have lived together but were inseparable since they have known each other, and that has been since the triplets were born. Harold and Fawn were married by the Seminole chief but never in a civil ceremony by the white law.

There is one more romance that was budding since the forest fire and the freeze even aided the two but they managed to keep it under the line of sight at the Tanner compound. Savannah and Chandler Jake Owen had been playing "patty fingers" for sometime now and no one really noticed, but Fawn had a keen eye for romance, Indian style and she saw through the avoiding glances and then a wink would give her the "for sure" signal that there was more than just a little friendly touch and hand holding out by the cow pens and an occasional glance.

This clandestine couple decided to go public with their romance and finally say yes to the love each shares with the other. They too wish to tie the knot on the same day as the other two making it a triple ring ceremony.

When they all told Maude Elsie at the same time, she said, "You've got to be kidding me! With three of my ladies getting married the same time, the same day, I will not bake each of you a wedding cake, you will have to do with one long cake divided up into three sections, whew! What a thing to put on me and now you all had better get busy and get this place decorated up the way you want it and I will call in Leona Petty, from Kissimmee to do the gowns and the bridesmaids dresses too. I have got to talk to Mary Remmick at Bent Penny as soon as possible."

Mary was such a willing helper and the other women came to the forefront too, to help Maude Elsie plan the wedding in the lobby of the Depot Boarding House. Blossom and Willie Mae took the chuck wagons out of the barn and drove them over to the Tanners that gave them extra cooking space and a place to sleep out of the summer weather, flying pests and serpents crawling on the ground. The other women who would help Maude Elsie, is Eunie Dunbar, Gladys Selmon, Birdy Ort and Hazelma "Dixie" Dicksey. Each of the ladies had a specific job to do and as the colorful day drew nearer the more nervous the brides got and the grooms at this point were taking all of this in stride and were doing what they could and helping to bring in barrels of beer, wine and filling the water pails with fresh water, as in the heat of the summer there was a lot of cool water being drunk.

The calliope was uncovered and brought out of the barn for the band to play and using the fold down stage gave a proper setting for the orchestra to sit and play with the calliope and the rest of the orchestra, the fiddles and brass with the drums, banjo, guitar, mandolin and the other bass string instruments and all could be played for the weddings.

A fire was started in the boiler and when the steam was up the calliope was played but was soft pedaled for the ocaision and the instrument sounded for all life like a pipe organ and was quickly adapted to the use of the musicians as a useful instrument, and it stood ready for the big day.

Taxdale Lightman the Circuit Judge was passing through and had dinner with the folks at the Depot Boarding House, he was pressed into use for writing the marriage licences for all three of the couples. Maude Elsie and Spurgeon were to be the Maid of honor and best man for all three. So the ceremony would flow and be over with all at the same time.

The minister from the First Baptist Church of Bartow was to officiate at the weddings. There would have to be a room for the brides to change in and one for the grooms to change in and one for the minister and his wife as- well-as the Judge. That was four rooms that could not be rented that week and if anyone more came and needed a room they would have to use the 14 X 9 (this was a tent that was kept for such emergencies) there were actually four of these tents and they were already erected in the dooryard all nice and neat and in line so that they looked for all the world like army tents which they were and Spurgeon bought them as surplus ten or fifteen years ago. Just last year the tents were taken down from the barn and bees wax and mineral oil were smeared on the fabric to make them more water resistant, as there is no such thing as a leak proof tent.

People were coming in their wagons and camping in them, others were bringing their own tents and tepees to shelter them for the duration of the festivities. The stable and stalls were full of horses and the coral was getting way too crowded as now the horses were beginning to kick and buck at other horses in the pen. The horses were taken to the pasture and let free to roam and graze as they wished, this opened the corral to the late comers who needed a place for their horses for a short stay as they would be leaving shortly after the ceremony and the feast, they would not wait for the couples to leave and be in the rice throwing.

A number of people stayed in their tents in the clearings near the Tanners Compound, as did the Seminole Indians who were also invited to the festivities. The days were getting fewer and the ladies of the house were getting nervous about the food preparation and if there would be enough or not.

They were surprised when the Indians came up near the back door near the kitchen, dug a pit put up a spit for roasting and the braves and the women started bringing up logs of oak, hickory, and citrus wood for the roasting fire. They started drying fish and quail, and doves for the feast and as they were dried they were stored in the smoke house where they would be flavored with the smoke house fire. Gator meat was also being dried and placed inside the smoke house but little of the gator meat remained when the feast was ready to be placed on the table.

The morning before the wedding two bucks were brought up. They had already been skinned and had the coat of salt, sugar, and other spices that the Indians used for the tenderizing the venison meat. The fire was not very high but was hot since the fire was started the evening before and tended all night until the coals were just right for the venison to be put on the spit and turned until the feast was read in the evening after the weddings.

A bushel of apples, a bushel of oranges, one of grapefruit, water melons, fried green tomatoes, potato salad, cucumber salad with sour cream, collard greens, green beans, baked beans, sweet potatoes, roast pork, ham, the fish, gator, and birds the Indians had dried. There was the venison, the roast beef was part of the spread, next came the desserts, the orange pies, key lime pies, lemon, apple, strawberry and pecan pies, angle food cake, vanilla yellow cake with chocolate icing, devils food cake with chocolate icing, coconut cake with white coconut icing. There were wash tubs full of sweet iced tea, pitchers of lemonade, orange juice, and ice water.

The more food brought out the more the tables groaned with the weight. The venison was being carved and the second buck had long since been on the spit and being turned with the fire still hot and the meat getting done for the people to feast on for as long as the food held out.

The orchestra was playing old favorites and the calliope was singing softly and it was indeed a good instrument to play with the orchestra. The piano was tuned and ready for the signal from the minister. The lobby and the kitchen was decorated with bay blossom magnolias, and other Florida flowers and swamp leather leaf ferns, gardenias were interwoven in the Spanish moss that was draped about the rooms. The ceremony would be at the front steps of the Depot Boarding House and the minister would stand on the porch while the brides and grooms stood on the ground just below the first porch step. The brides maid and best man stood behind the three couples to hand the grooms the rings when the minister asked for them. The brides were given away by Judge Taxdale Lightman.

At four o'clock sharp Mary Remmick started playing the piano and at four - 0- five she started playing the wedding march, and the three ladies started up the path to the front steps where their men were waiting. The Judge escorted the three brides to the altar and when asked,

"Who giveth these ladies in Holy Matrimony?" The Judge said, "I do." then he stepped back and stood behind the men with Spurgeon there as their best man.

Joe "Mossy Back" Tuttle and Efrim Johnson the stagecoach drivers for Spurgeon had long since watched the whole thing from the side of the house and were weaving back and forth in the afternoon Florida summer sun, they had possibly been into the swamp juice but they were not usually one who would have a drink or two before an event such as this. Hans Nuddleman the owner of the sawmill and his wife were standing in the crowd, and watched as the rings were given to the brides and then to the grooms. Doctor Montague Zimmerman and his daughter were there because he wanted his daughter who was now nineteen years to perhaps get the marriage bug, and get married to her boy friend in Bartow. The whole household came from the Bent Penny Ranch, and stayed for the meal, there was Jeremiah Coxin, Earl Ray and Mary Remmick, Tom and Blossom with their children Billy and Little Mary, Billy Matson the freight driver from the Bent Penny, and sheriff Mel Melrose, Davy, Brittany and the twins. All in all there were over one hundred people there to the wedding and the feast afterward.

The Saturday before all the men went to Bartow to the barber shop and got a hair cut, shave and shampoo. The men had to pay the barber seventy-five cents each for the tonsorial procedure that made them look and feel a whole lot cleaner and neater for the wedding. Mossy Back and Efrim were in town and watched the whole thing through the barber shop window, ocaisionally glancing at each other in disbelief.

The wedding vows now over and the brides and grooms having been introduced to the onlookers, went to their special rooms to change into their traveling clothes and get ready for the meal to follow and to cut the wedding cakes.

The crowd started filing into the kitchen where the food was on the table and the chairs and stools, barells, and a few stumps were what the folks sat on to eat their meal out of doors. After the line had finished there were those who wanted more food and swept back into the dining room for seconds. Anyone who left hungry was their own fault. And there were even plates that would be eaten later in the evening so the people were fed and the dirty dishes, bowls, pots and pans had to be washed, the women all pitched in, and even the Indian women and soon the dishes were washed dried, and put away. The abundant amount of scraps left over were fed to the hogs, any meat, bones or meat scraps were put out for the dogs to eat. The flowers and decorations were given to the wedding guests, to take along with them to their homes, tents, or camping wagons, there were some sweet smelling abodes that night.

The three couples were carried in the stagecoach with Mossy Back and Efrim driving them to Ft. Cummins, there they all caught the midnight train to Sanford where they boarded the steam boat to Jacksonville for a week, then back home and to their own jobs.

Claude had three people to train as the tracks to Fort Meade were now finished and the train was going along and now Western Union needed more telegraphers.

Life settled back into the old groove that existed before the wedding and the days of the week were filled with Monday washing, Tuesday ironing, Wednesday baking, Thursday cleaning, Friday change bed linens, Saturday, shopping, barber shop, and mending, Sunday, Sunday school and church.

And so it went week after week until someone gets married, has a child, goes away or dies. The days all fall to the same job depending on the day of the week, the job had to be finished for the next week will be around before they know it.

LONG DAYS AND HARD WORK

The weddings were over and now with the three women on their honeymoon, Maude Elsie found the going really tough even with Dixie, Eunie, Gladys, and Birdy, there was a large hole in the service department with all the work that had to be done at the Depot Boarding House. Monday the washing had to be done and without Harold to chop wood the chore fell on the shoulders of Ski and Norm, however they kept the wood boxes filled and wood chopped for the next go round.

Tuesday came, the ironing and the kitchen stove was ready with the flat irons on the plate heating and the ironing boards set up this day, only three ironing boards were at the ready. More than once the women thanked God that they weren't still putting up the white table clothes for the linemen. The ironing would never be done before supper time, as it would not this day and the supper would possibly be left overs from the wedding still as there was some smoked deer and fish left but no vegetables, biscuits, gravy or pecan pie, so if the men wanted ironed clothes they would just have to scrape for them selves this supper time.

Finally at ten o'clock in the evening the last piece was folded and the irons placed on the cooling tin in back of the stove where the iron never got cold but stayed warm in case there was a last minute touch up that had to be done an iron would be heated and ready in just a few minutes. These little emergencies arose every day and sometimes twice.

Wednesday, the flour and lard, yeast and buttermilk all displayed on the pie safe and the bakers pantry, both of which stood on the opposite wall from the stove, there was an island in the middle of the kitchen and this is where the children usually were when the women were cooking or baking. There was an extra amount of dough sitting on the island warming and rising. This was for a special treat in the morning at breakfast. Maude Elsie will be frying yeast donuts for the men in the morning.

The bread was baking and cakes and pies were being put together while the bread baked and the next batch was rising. As soon as the last batch of bread was baked and out of the oven the pies went in and the women would stand on the ironing porch to get any breeze at all that would blow through the screens on three sides of the porch. Maude Elsie would pick up her apron and wipe her face and by the time the apron was dropped her face was popped out with sweat again. The other three ladies were the same way as they each went to the linen drawer and pulled out a clean, dry apron. As the day of baking drew to a close the supper meal was already started and it would take only about one half hour more to have the meal on the table.

Ski, dropped the load of wood he had in his arms and went back out the back door, picked up the steel bar and started ringing the dinner bell, when they saw the small party of Indians riding up into the dooryard.

They dropped a body on the ground and dismounted. The Chief Leo Two Feathers, went to the Western Union office, the other Indians brought the body up to the porch and laid the remains of a man on the porch, then wrapped him in an old blanket. The man was apparently dead of one gun shot wound to the heart. Spurgeon noticed that the Indians had no guns with them and he didn't notice whether the chief had a gun on him or not. As Spurgeon walked into the telegraphers office the chief was asking for sheriff Mel to talk on the talking wire for him to know who the dead man was.

Norm Tracy was the telegrapher and he was learning the trade from Claude on his off time and between chores, but Spurgeon never had to tell Norm to go back to work as Spurgeon wanted him to learn and even gave this time off so he could fill in for Claude while he was away on his honeymoon.

In about thirty minutes sheriff Melrose answered the query from Norm at the depot.

"Who is the dead man that the chief has brought in?" the telegraph clicked and clacked until the transmission was over.

"We do not know who the man is." answered Chief Leo Two Feathers, then continued, "we found him at the cypress well and he had lost a lot of blood and he died."

"Is he a white man?" the sheriff asked.

"Yes," came the terse answer from the chief

"Was there anything in his pockets?" the sheriff asked.

The chief went out side and said something to the Indians in Seminole, and they started to go through his pockets, and, there was a piece of paper, a pocket knife, a comb and a wallet with five hundred dollars in it.

The chief told all of this to the sheriff and waited for the answer.

"Give the money to Spurgeon and look for any identification on the man.

The chief went back to the Indians and told them that they needed to identify the man. They all shook their heads and then they took his boots off and in the left boot they found a name and address: one, Jesse Pollard Winthrop, of Fort Meade, Florida.

The sheriff said, "Well tell Chief Leo Two Feathers that he was wanted for armed robbery of the State Bank in Ft. Meade, and the men at the bank thought they had shot at and hit him, but were not sure. And thank the Chief for his civic duty so well preformed, he will get ten percent of the money he turns into the bank and he can keep fifty dollars of the money and Spurgeon can lock the balance in his safe until I can get there,"

Norm wrote the message out and handed a copy of it to the chief then tapped out, "N.T.T.D.G.N." (Norm Tracy, at Tanners Depot, Good Night).

The Indian braves were already digging a hole in the scrub near where the young man was buried and two of the gang that didn't make it to jail the second time so it was a bad mans grave yard.

It was time to eat supper now and the Indians came in after the burial and sat at the table with the others and ate. Finding the white man's food to their liking one of the men wanted to send his squaw to learn to "cook white."

After supper Spurgeon counted the fifty dollars out into the hand of the chief, the chief took the money and placed it into a buckskin wallet and stuck the wallet into his blue jeans pocket and said, "good bye," to the folks and shook hands with Spurgeon and they rode off into the scrub not to be heard from again for a while.

"What do you think of our bad man's graveyard out there in the Scrub?" Maude Elsie asked Spurgeon.

"Well, ah haint thot 'bout hit atall, they's jist alyin thar not doin no harm ta nobody atall now and most uv'm is been worth sum bounty money so's ah caint fuss nun 'bout at thar atall. Hit seem a mite stuck in yur craw some what choo got agin them thar dead fellers you wont em dug up an putt in tha swamp fer the gators, um, ah mean whot you got a idear you jist let me know no how an ah'll get them Indians ta dig em up an put em somer's else a tuther then." Spurgeon answered then looked away from Maude Elsie as Dixie walked into the kitchen where Maude Elsie and Spurgeon were talking.

"My goodness I thought this day would never end so I could get cleaned up and get on toward home," Dixie said in a chatty voice to anyone and no one in particular for it was just something to say as she swished through the kitchen grabbing her wrap and a bag of left overs from supper and went back out of the door she came into the kitchen by. Maude Elsie nor Spurgeon had an opportunity to speak even a word to her she made her entrance and exit so quickly.

"Dixie," Maude Elsie called behind her and she was already on the front porch when she turned and answered through the screen door.

"Yes maam," she replied.

"Can you come in at four thirty in the morning, it will be Tuesday and we are behind in our ironing. Bring anyone else who might want to make a few pennies for the day. We really need to get the ironing done, as Wednesday will be another long day because we have to bake extra bread and desserts for the Adams'es, she hasn't been able to do anything since the new baby was born. That makes nine children she and her husband have, I don't have to ask what they do in their spare time." Maude Elsie called back through the kitchen and waited for an answer but there was none for she had been talking to an empty screen door since the words "four thirty."

Spurgeon said, "You haint give me no answer bout them daid men out'n the scrub and I still don know whut choo wonts ta said bout hit no how," finishing with a chuckle.

"Spurgeon you do what you want to do about the situation. I just wish they were not so near our compound and . . ." Maude Elsie decided that she was wasting her breath so she just stopped talking about it.

Spurgeon was goading his wife and in jest he said, "Mebby ah'll putt a fence 'round at aire graveyard an when people cum roun' cheer ah'll charge em a nickle ta go an look at them thar graves, cept ah aint got a foggy idear who is buried whar, course hit don't make no never mind as who be buried whar, cuz them folks'll jist be a lookin at the graves no how, . . . Maude Elsie you thank a nickle bees enough?"

"You hush, you old jack leg, go twist the cow's tail not mine." Maude Elsie said back to Spurgeon as she walked out of the kitchen with the coal oil lamp, leaving him in the dark room alone.

Just as Spurgeon and Maude Elsie were about to get into bed there came a knock on the door of the lobby, which was closed at night but never locked incase someone needed a room and they could as the sign says "LOOK IN THE MAIL BOXES, IF THERE IS A KEY, THEN GO TO THAT ROOM AND REGISTER IN THE MORNING WHEN WE ARE UP. BREAKFAST IS AT SIX O'CLOCK AM. TANNERS"

The knock came again, so Spurgeon slipped into his trousers and went to the door. He opened the door and there was sheriff Mel.

"What choo doin out this time o night sheriff?" Spurgeon asked then added, "We aint got no vacancy's we is all full up.

"I came to check out the Indian's story and to collect the five hundred dollars less the fifty you gave the chief," the sheriff said to Spurgeon. Then added, "I was hoping you would have a room cause I am about as tired as a man can be and still be breathing."

"I tell you whut choo kin do, you kin stay in one uv them chuck wagons outside them's gots a bed and all and the feller from the Bent Penny Ranch haint come an got em yet so sleep in one o them an hit wont cost the county nuthin then don't cha know." Spurgeon told the sheriff, who turned and went outside and into one of the chuck wagons for the night.

Spurgeon turned down the hall lamp and went to bed, Maude Elsie was already asleep.

Spurgeon lay beside her listening to her even breathing until he dropped off to sleep.

Four thirty found Maude Elsie and Spurgeon sitting at the table eating and drinking coffee when Billy Matson walked in and told them he was about to take the two chuck wagons out of their dooryard but was told to sit down and eat breakfast or at least have a cup of coffee.

Dixie was on time and with her were two black ladies and Maude Elsie recognized one of them and said, "Willie Lou why, haven't I thought of you before now," and went and hugged the rotund lady, who shook all over when she laughed.

"Mizz Spurgeon you knows I aint been around dees parts fer some spell now, Ize been ta At-Lanter a visitin my little "Cooter" girl, she bees in a school up thar she gonna be a nurse when she gad gee ates fum that school up thar, you know that?" Willie Lou shouted as she always did talk too loud and was "shushed" just about all the time when she was talking for a long time.

"I had no idea that Caroline was even out of highschool. I know you are proud of her, I know I am for you," Maude Elsie made over the young girls success.

"And who is this that you have brought with you Willie Lou?" Maude Elsie asked before the black lady could start talking again.

"Mizz Spurgeon, at aire bees mah tuther baby, Shiella, she didn't wont ta goat ta no mo school she say she done has enough learnin to tide her over fer a spell so she hep me now in a again, lack today when you needs mo hep than you gots folks ta do tha work," Willie Lou said in her loud voice.

Soon breakfast was done and the dishes washed, dried, and put away the four women started on the ironing and by supper time had finished.

Meanwhile the two chuck wagons were on their way back to the Bent Penny Ranch.

25

A Trip Over The Bent Penny Trace

The chuck wagons rumbled down the clay paving of the Bent Penny Trace, though it was not daylight yet the lead wagon pulled over to the side of the road and pulled the team up. Billy Matson pulled up behind the other wagon and shouted, "What's up John Henry?"

"Ahm cold and I'ma gonna built a far and make coffee, you wont sumpin else?" John Henry shouted back.

"Yeah, ah wonts some bacon n beans I could et at the Tanners but ah wont ta git on toward the Bent Penny," Billy spoke in a loud voice.

While in the woods as they were most of the time if a bear is around he wont come into the camp if it is noisy.

Soon the fire was licking the darkness back into the scrub, it was heating the coffee pot, the skillet for the bacon and John Henry.

The bacon frying and the coffee boiling make a wonderful aroma in the early morning and today was no exception. But for the rustle of a flap on one of the chuck wagons being folded back and a very sleepy and surprised sheriff Mel, Melrose came around the wagon to the fire.

"I didn't heer no hoss cum up didju John Henry?" Billy Matson asked,

"No sir I aint heard no hoss cum up ta here on us, Billy," John Henry exclaimed.

"Sheriff whot is you a doin outcheer this time a mawnin?" Billy Matson asked.

"Well, I went to sleep in the bed of that chuck wagon and I guess everybody forgot about me being in there," the sheriff answered.

"Well, sheriff do you thank we should oughta taken you back ta the Tanners?" Asked John Henry.

"Go ahead and laugh you two knot heads I know you all are about to bust a gut holding back on a joke like this one," the sheriff began to laugh and soon they all were doubled over with laughter.

Hoof beats were heard and the three stepped back into the shadows, and soon a rider with an extra horse was seen coming down the trace in the morning light.

"I thank that bees mista Spurgeon. Hit sit in tha saddle lack him," John Henry exclaimed.

"Yeah ats who tiz alright enough and he a leaden the sheriff's mare too. Look lack we aint gonna git back ta tha Tannerses," Billy said as Spurgeon rode up and alit by the campfire.

"Ah'm shore sorry Mel I didn't know that the boys had taken the chuck wagons until I looked outside and they weren't there no more. And I knowed you was in one of em. So I hurried up and saddled our horses and run down here after you all. I am mighty lucky at John Henry wanted ta git warm an drank sum coffee, don't cha know" Spurgeon explained and apologized at the same time.

Needless to say, the secret of the missing sheriff created much laughter in Bartow, and the little Blue Plate Café where the sheriff ate most of his meals and of course charged them to the county.

"I aint been so hume-a-lated a fore in my whole life as I was when I woke up in that chuck wagon and smelled coffee and bacon, I looked out through the flap in the cover and seen John Henry an Billy Matson out aire a cookin vittles an coffee. And bout that time I woulda give My grand daddy's coonskin hat fer a cup of coffee anyhow." The sheriff touted as he told the story of being kidnaped, "by . . . by such as The Black Bandit and Dangerous Billy the mule skinner, Matson." and the sheriff would roar in laughter.

The Bartow Democrat, picked up on the story and printed the story about the sheriff being kidnaped by the two dangerous desperados who just happened to take the sheriff for a ride.

Soon the whole county was reading and laughing at the story that started out as "The Incident at Tanners Depot."

The women thought that the incident was totally over played and soon the news paper was being used to clean lamp chimneys of all the suet. A few of them sent the used paper to the sheriff without a return address.

Maude Elsie and Dixie, Eunie, Gladys, Birdy, Willie Lou and her daughter Shiella, had all the work on themselves what with the other women on their honeymoon. The quantity nor the quality of the food coming from the kitchen was not the problem. The problem was the cleaning of the rooms. Now that there was only two women to make the beds of the rooms which were rented to transients were the last to be made up and as a result it was past the four o'clock pm check in time that the rooms were finished with a fresh made bed, clean towels and a pitcher full of fresh water beside the washbasin on the toilet cabinet. In the summer the windows were left open and with the cross ventilation and the copula in the center of the roof under the stairwell, kept the breeze coming into the room with a little puff of the sheer curtains. A coal oil lamp stood on the dresser and two on either side of the mirror on the toilet cabinet. Candles were also available to avoid the excess heat in the summer time.

Those who were full time guests had the linens changed every Thursday and if fresh towels were needed cost an extra five cents for every extra towel and pillow case. For extra sheets the cost was seven cents. The amount of money that was charged had little to do with the amount it cost to do the laundry, rather, to discourage the miss use of the linen service where there were usually only enough to make it from Monday to Monday and wash day.

If a sheet or pillow case got torn they were used for dish towels or torn into stripe for bandages. The kitchen help were always cutting their fingers and having to bandage them, the men would cut themselves with an axe or other sharp instrument, a horse or a mule would have a sensitive leg or a sprain and would need a wrap and some liniment to aid healing. Nothing was wasted, there was a saying, "Use it up, wear it out, make do or do without," this principal was taken to heart and was part of everyday living in the scrubs of central Florida.

Maude Elsie and Mary Sykes Remmick had to re-think the order of sugar and coffee since the passing of Chief Billy Bow Legs, as the new chief, Chief Leo Two Feathers drank only a cup of coffee when he visited the Bent Penny Ranch or the Depot, and that was usually for trading for what ever was available, mostly salt from the ranch and other foods from the depot and general store.

The gator hide barrel kept moving further and further away from the front door of the general store. Those hides stunk to high heaven and were taken to Tampa once a month just to please the women who traded at the general store. For some of the women who would smell the hides as they passed by the barrel would have the "vapors" when they came into the store and the smelling salts were broken out to revive the poor soul. Others would hold their breath and rush past the stinking container as they entered the store. Summer time was the worse time of the year as the hides would "cure" faster in the blazing Florida heat and cause the barrels to be moved a bit further away.

There was a time when the breeze changed and the diners at the depot had to endure the aroma of the gator hide barrel for several days, it took about two weeks for the regular diners to filter back in and enjoy the food and the aroma of the kitchen without the stench of salted gator hides invading the tender pallets of the diners at the depot. At that time the hides were relegated to the space behind the barn, but even the animals would complain about the bad smell all the night long.

New things kept arriving in the general store as Maude Elsie bending to her own wishes ordered a barrel of soda crackers from the wholesaler. It wasn't even making a print in the floor when the men started calling each other soda crackers and not Florida crackers anymore. It made Maude Elsie mad enough to get rid of the soda crackers and the hogs had a squealing, hogging banquet out of the several thousands of soda crackers.

Another new thing came in the catalog and that was new kitchen equipment, the new coal oil stoves would guarantee anyone to keep the kitchen cooler from the heat, a large ice box to hold three hundred pounds of ice were only a couple of things that were offered and Maude Elsie decided she wanted the coal oil stove just to keep the heat from the kitchen. The package came while she was picking black berries down by the swamp, so Spurgeon, Mossy Back and Efrim all unloaded it from the freight wagon and had the new stove sitting in the place of the wood stove, which was relegated to the front porch.

The supper meal was cooked and eaten by the diners and for the first time in the history of the Depot Boarding House, there were leftovers and a lot of them. The next morning Maude Elsie and Willie Lou were cooking breakfast on the wood stove on the porch and not complaining as the open porch was way better than the enclosed kitchen. But the coal oil stove was sent to the blacksmith shop for boiling glue and heating pitch for saddle repair. It worked well for that as the aroma of the sinew in the glue was surpassed only by the smell of the coal oil stove. And it didn't make any difference as to the taste of the two adhesives.

One day one of the men got the hot pitch and tried to grease a wagon wheel with the sticky mess. The smithy worked all day the next day tryin to get the wheel off of the wagon without doing in the hub and the wheel. At long last a fire was built on the ground and when it was roaring hot the wheel was put on the fire which left only the iron tire from the wagon wheel, all else had been consumed by the fire when the grease caused the pitch to catch up and fire consumed the wheel hub where with cold water only the wooden rim and the iron tire were all that was really salvageable. The wheel wright and the smithy spent the whole day repairing the wheel that should have taken only fifteen minutes to grease and replace it on the wagon.

FOR EVER IN THE SCRUB

It was past four thirty in the morning, Spurgeon had been up for about fifteen minutes as he made his way back from the outhouse to the wash stand beside the kitchen door. Looking through the window he noticed that there was no light in the kitchen as Maude Elsie should have been there at least lighting the fire in the wood stove and getting ready for breakfast. There was no one in the kitchen. Spurgeon walked over and entered their bed room expecting to see Maude Elsie sitting on the side of the bed trying to work the nights sleep from her brain. This time she was still in her bed as though she had not heard the alarm clock wind down its two bell ringer.

She had not stirred. Spurgeon lit the coal oil lamp beside the bed and turned the covers back to see Maude Elsie staring back at him with sightless, dead eyes.

Spurgeon gasped as he knew that the love of his life had slipped from the bonds of the earth and the scrub sometime during the night.

Spurgeon in a daze went to Savannah and Jake Owens' room, knocked on the door then called, "Savannah!" could . . . could youens come an hep me? I thank Maude Elsie bees daid . . . I . . . don't know whut ta do now."

Savannah and Jake appeared almost instantly at the door and took Spurgeon by the hand and led him to the kitchen. Jake went to the room where Maude Elsie laid and found that it was true, she was indeed dead. He touched her cold arm and as he did he shuddered all over his body, then he stepped out of the room and went to Claude and Nadine's room where he knocked on the door and when Claude answered he told him what was wrong. Claude woke Nadine and they went to the kitchen to be with Spurgeon, who was sitting in his chair at the head of the table and just staring at the empty chair which would be for Maude Elsie, that is when she would sit down. She was usually serving someone else and her chair would be empty until everyone of her guests, and what she called her family, had finished their meal. She would sit and eat her food and drink her cup of cold coffee.

There was an air that was hanging over the Depot Boarding House, and as each of the guests arose and slipped into the kitchen were greeted with the sad news of the death of Maude Elsie. Somehow the death did not fit the time as there was too much to do and to few to do the work. Now there was one less to do the chores around the Tanners settlement.

Hardly anyone could believe that Maude Elsie was not coming into the kitchen and making the biscuits dough while the stove was heating and as it did the coffee was to boil. Yet this morning it was daylight before the stove was heated as Nadine and Savannah got the morning's breakfast started. The biscuits were in the oven, the bacon was frying, grits were cooking, and soon the eggs would be in the skillet, and breakfast would be placed on the table.

Ski would suddenly disappear into the scrub and would not reappear until a day later when he brought in a beautiful casket made from a single cypress tree, the lining was from the material the Indians had sewn together and the many colors suited Maude Elsie's clothes which she was to be laid to rest in. Her graying hair was done up into the bun that she always wore and on her hand were the wedding rings she cherished so.

Spurgeon had given her the rings when they took a trip to Jacksonville about ten years ago and she was so surprised that she sat and wept. Spurgeon thought he had done something wrong and was feeling very uneasy about the gift until she reached and hugged him in her arms and kissed him on his lips. Then and only then did he know that he was not in trouble and kissed her back.

The black folks who lived near by were there and the Indians as was many of the guest of the past years who had known Maude Elsie and loved her. Most of the people from the Bent Penny Ranch had come by and were getting ready for the funeral.

Spurgeon had gone to the area he had cleared for Maude Elsie to sit and listen to the scrub she loved so dearly. He had gone there and dug her grave and had Claude telegraph the stone cutter in Kissimmee, to have the stone as soon as he could deliver it to the settlement.

The pastor from the First Baptist Church, in Bartow and Chief Leo Two Feathers officiated over the funeral and Maude Elsie, Tanner, was laid to rest as she would always be a woman in the scrub, the long days and hard work were behind her now, and she knew from early on that Spurgeon would be well cared for with the love that Savannah and Nadine had for the aging widower.

After the funeral and everyone had walked by the grave and paid their respects to the family, they went to the kitchen where the tables were again weighed down with food and drink of all kinds. The best part of the whole thing was how the people visited and talked to one another, the mood was not gay nor somber, just life in the scrub. The children ran about the dooryard and an occasional shout from a concerned mother, "Play nice and don't get you clothes dirty."

With all the talking, eating, visiting and generally getting acquainted and reacquainted, this was still a working farm too. Cows had to be milked, eggs gathered, animals fed and bedded for the night. Water pumped and brought in for the breakfast and for drinking during the night if anyone got thirsty.

The stove was getting colder and it was time to place the yeast dough on the back of the stove to rise during the night to be ready for yeast donuts the next morning. This was a special treat for the children, but only if thy were good little boys and girls.

Spurgeon watched as the sun set and the darkness started to inch its way into the scrub and try as he might he could not make this day last any longer, so he gave up his burden and walked to the house. His shoulders were slumped and his head would not stay erect as he passed folks who would pat him on the back and wish him well. He thanked them but did not see their faces, he walked into the kitchen and asked for a cup of coffee and a glass of water, his appetite for food had not returned.

Ski, Owen, Claude and Nadine saw to the chores in the barn, as Spurgeon never gave them a thought as he stared at the empty chair beside him at the table.

It was long after midnight that Spurgeon stirred and then stood up, as he did he felt weak and confused he tried to find his room and was told to go under the stairs, at which point he walked into Claude and Nadine's room. Claude rose and led him to his bedroom where he laid on the bed without removing any of his clothing. Claude went and called Nadine who helped him remove his clothes and tucked him in under the covers. Nadine leaned down and kissed the Patriarch on the forehead, turned down the lamp and left the room. She left the door ajar so they could hear if he started to roam about in the night.

The next morning found Spurgeon had started the fire in the stove and had the coffee on and ready to boil. He was not much of a hand in the kitchen but on a cattle drive he was a passable cook. His trail hand culinary fare was usually bacon, beans, dough biscuits, jam and coffee, that was pretty much what the guests found when they came down to the kitchen for their breakfast this morning.

Each guest spoke to Spurgeon as he went about serving the plates and saying, "Ah miss Maude Elsie as she would usually have this done by now . . . ah jist been too slow and she would fuss at me . . . Lord, hows ah done wants ta heard at aire 'gain."

Spurgeon turned and went to get the coffee pot but he met Savannah, with it in her hand already.

Dixie steered him to his chair at the table and as he sat down she patted him on the shoulder.

This mornings breakfast was eaten in silence as there was little to talk about and the small talk would be about the funeral, the people who attended, and the meal afterward with nothing to say, nothing was said.

"Oh yalls caint not talk ta one a tuther? Hits lack a grave yard in here, now youens please talk 'bout sumpin so's hit aint so quiet in here," Spurgeon spoke up after while and admonished the folks there at the breakfast table. Then they started talking, but the din at the table was neither gay nor somber, as they continued eating. Soon the meal was over and coffee cups were refilled once more before the chores of the day get started.

Billy Matson drove up in his freight wagon, he had a crate from the stone cutter in Kissimmee, and it was taken to the grave site where the men wrestled it off the wagon and placed at the head of Maude Elsie's grave. The wide pink marble stone read, "Maude Elsie Tanner, 1834-1899, rest in His arms." Spurgeon read it and, he wept.

HAIL TO THE TWENTIETH CENTURY

The year 1901 has brought great changes to the scrub. The Bent Penny Trace has become a major thoroughfare and is maintained by the road crew from Bartow, and kept up by the Polk County Road Department. There is now one hundred miles of clay-paved roads in Polk County and the road to Fort Clinch and on to Fort Meade has become the north - south highway with the most traffic still going south, as the population seems to be shifting to south Florida. As the east coast of Florida builds into more than fishing villages, some major ports have sprung out of the wilderness in south Florida. The cow catching has also moved and left the scrubs bare of the wild Florida cattle, the Marsh Tackie horse, and the wild catch dogs.

In the case of the dogs, they were either tamed and brought into the homes and ranches of central Florida or have been hunted and killed because of the dogs hunting in packs like wolves, killing new born calves, sheep and goats. They have been found to carry the disease hydro-phobia, a disease which has killed many a dog, cat, opossum, fox, wolf, and coyote all over Florida.

The railroad is now a web of transportation all through Florida. Goods are shipped from here to places up north. The produce crops are abounding because of the new refrigerated cars with ice bunkers and fans to keep the products cool and moist. They arrive in Chicago in three days and New York in two days, according to the advertisements in the newspapers and the "Saturday Evening Post."

The Florida Crackers are now seldom just cracker cowboys, but are ranchers and ranch hands, and have seen the cattle bred with, Hereford, Brahma, and the American Bison, which was short lived as the domestic cow could not birth the large buffalo calf. The loss of the cow left the orphan calf, half buffalo and half domestic cow with Hereford ancestry, was too much of a gamble for the ranchers to take. The breeding program with the American Bison was dropped.

There was still enough pioneer spirit left in the people and they still used the Almanac for the farmers planting, ranchers breeding, and health information, like a bible and it settled an awful lot of arguments.

By this time in the twentieth century the average life expectancy in the U. S. was forty-seven years, there were only eight thousand automobiles and one hundred fourty miles of asphalt paved roads. There were now speed limits of ten miles per hour and this included people on horseback. Sugar cost four cents a pound, eggs were fourteen cents a dozen, coffee cost fifteen cents a pound. Some of the leading causes of death were pneumonia and influenza, tuberculosis, heart attack, and stroke. The American flag now had forty-five stars.

Spurgeon was still living at the Depot Boarding House though the general store had burned two years ago and another was built in its place. The Depot was saved mostly by the new Florida Forest services pumper steam engine which was now at the barn in the Tanner Settlement. The steam was kept up and when there was a fire, the wood was piled into the firebox and the horses hooked up, then away they would go. At the fire a hose was dropped into a pond or in the case of the general store, the well. Valves were turned and the engine began pumping the water from the well through the fire hoses and onto the fire. By the time the engine was rolled out and the water was pumping through the hoses, about five hundred to one thousand gallons of water was pumped from the well and that was all of the water the engine could pump, and the people just stayed and watched it burn to the ground. Some things were saved and some nonessentials were left in the store to be consumed by the blaze.

Spurgeon spent a lot of time now with his three sons who came back home, Seth was going to the University of Florida in Ocala and Gainesville. Thomas had spent twenty years in the U. S. Yankee Army and had a retirement of fifty dollars a month. Spurgeon the Third was up in north Florida working in a pine tar and terpentine still to learn the trade.

Spurgeon would watch as his namesake took charge of the new still which was up and running at the Tanner settlement.

Seth started running the businesses and found the Depot Boarding House was the most difficult to organize due to the amount of sheets and other linens that were here, there and yonder. The food was being taken from the store without accounting for the Depot kitchen. He really inherited a mess.

Thomas stood by and watched until he found to his amazement there was a one hundred year old stagecoach in the barn and a steam driven calliope. These antiques piqued his curiosity and he began restoring the stagecoach first. The wheels were taken to the wheelwright at the Bent Penny Ranch and the seats inside and out, had to be recovered. Gallons of varnish and a lot of sanding soon gave way to the wonderful Tanner Stage Line coach, all new and shiny. Thomas asked his dad about the harnessing and even horses. Spurgeon went to the barn with him and soon old harness was coming alive with the addition of saddle soap and neats foot oil. Spurgeon warned him about the expense of keeping eight pulling horses and how much it would take to train four teams to pull as one team, and he thought he was up to the job. The following Saturday Spurgeon and his three sons hooked up the buggy and rode to Plant City to the cow and horse auction. They looked and only one team was auctioned off, but they would not be suitable for the stagecoach because they were too small and were more for the light buggy or a buckboard wagon. Weeks went by and they were able to get three teams, when Spurgeon's son, Spurgeon the Third, the other brothers called him "Pigeon" and so shall we from this time forward.

Pigeon heard of a team in Kissimmee which had been pulling a freight wagon and were about eighteen hands high, big enough to team with the stage. The Tanner men went to Kissimmee and were seen on their way home with the team of horses tied to the rear of the wagon. Soon there were four stout teams first of all hitched to the four-in-hand team with the newest team as lead. The second team and the third team apparently were accustomed to either leading or being the only team on a pull. They gave them a bit of a problem until Spurgeon told Thomas to separate the two teams and let one team be first pull nearest the stagecoach, the second team was the original fourth team, second from the stagecoach. The third pull was third in line and the newest as lead team. They would hardly do what the commands said with just walking around the area, so Spurgeon suggested that they hitch them up to a stump that was half way dug out and needed a good pull to jerk out of the ground.

The skidding tongs were attached to the stump and the four teams hitched to the tongs.

Spurgeon cracked his whip and the horses all pulled as one. The stump did not have a chance. It snapped and gave a groan of some type but came out of the hole without even a small amount of pressure from the team. Thomas walked around and shouted orders to the team to gee and haw, to whoa, giddy up and finally back up. The teams needed no more training than that and as the stump was duly placed at the wood pile to be sawn up and used as fat-lightered pine, this great team of teams were hitched to the stagecoach.

Mossy Back Tuttle and Efrim Johnson had been watching the show from their cabin across from the barn where they collected the five cents for the tourists to look at the graves of the outlaws shot and buried at the settlement. The two wanted to sit in the seat of the brand new stage just once more and were willing helpers at the hitching of the team to the stage.

Thomas looked at Mossy Back and asked, "You know anything about how to drive one of these things?"

"Yes sir, ah thank ah kin mos lackly make her go and make her whoa, iffen yall wonts me ta." then Mossy Back added, "ah dun whuped at aire stage bout a zillion miles thru ish here scrub, me an Efrim here can even make her fly lack weuns did onect affore. Course when we lit hit busted the two front wheels frum under us when hit come down."

Efrim was looking at Thomas with fear and dread in his eyes and thought that Spurgeon would fire the both of them if he felt they had tried to make the stage fly that day on the trail, but Spurgeon knew what had happened and was laughing as Mossy Back finished his story.

"Okay then Mossy Back, you climb up in the box with me and teach me to drive an eight- in-hand team, will you please." asked Thomas.

The team pulled the stagecoach flawlessly and it was a race to see who was going to ride in the new stagecoach.

The next was the calliope and soon Pigeon had all the brass polished and the red on the wagon repainted and the entire music wagon ready to roll. The original pair of black horses had died of old age, but the team was just as willing to pull the music wagon, and away it went along with the stagecoach to fairs and rodeos and conventions around the county and from time to time appeared in parades in Tampa and Orlando.

The naval stores located around central Florida were changing fast and going the way of the rest of the unspoiled land. Now large real estate firms were buying up the government land, putting up fences and in some cases sub-dividing the property to sell small lots for building houses. The land was not being used for farming, ranching, or for cutting timber, nor slashing the pines for their valuable sap to make tar, pitch and terpentine. Like many other gems in the jeweled crown of Florida industries, these fences have cut off the growth for these small islands to be special in the large scheme of Florida growth.

Seth Tanner was using the growth that included the land which was owned by the Tanners, the folks at the Bent Penny Ranch and their many acres of land still dotted with stands of yellow pines, to the individual who had only a few trees in the homestead. Each tree was another drop in the sap bucket. When the trees could no longer be tapped for terpentine, they could be sawn for lumber for now trees were worth as much as five dollars to the sawmill. The sawmill had to keep running to make money and to make money the miller had to sell lumber. With the building of houses and the cross ties used by the railroad, the trees were thinning in the woods around this part of Florida.

Land was cleared and citrus was planted. There was now a trade for the citrus fruit which went to market on the trains that rolled on tracks spiked to the crossties that were pine trees straight and tall only a few months ago. Progress was making the persons who had the ideas and the ability to make things out of the wilderness and beat the wilderness back to form towns, municipalities, and settlements out of the scrub, paved roads from cow trails. Freshly cleared land becoming farms of pineapples, sugarcane, tomatoes, cabbages, strawberries, pumpkins, squash and watermelons. What wasn't consumed locally was shipped up north or out west or to a thousand other hamlets, settlements, towns and cities. With railroads spanning the United States of America like a giant spider spinning its web, the trains moved, and when they moved, they took with them success from one place and some of what was made, grown or dug up was sent back to the needs of central Florida.

None of this could have been accomplished anywhere in the world or the U.S.A., had it not been for the women who bore the young, made the gardens, cooked the food, washed the clothes, milked the cows, ironed the clothes, taught the schools, kept the home and hearth so the men who were still hunter and gatherers at this time could come home to a hot meal, clean cabin, clean sheets and well mannered and educated children. All this progress was possible because of WOMEN IN THE SCRUB and their LONG DAYS AND HARD WORK.

THE END, AND A BEGINNING

Printed in the United States
By Bookmasters